RAVEN ROUSTING
A SHIFTER SEEKER NOVELLA

HEATHER McCORKLE

Raven Rousting
A Shifter Seeker Novella

Copyright 2022 Heather McCorkle

Paperback ISBN: 978-1-939469-07-6
eBook ISBN: 978-1-939469-08-3

Cover images from Thinkstock. Cover design by McCorkle Creations.

First Edition.

Compass Press release date: 5/30/2022

Recommended Reading Order:

The Children of Fenrir Series:
Clawed & Cornered (novella)
Bitten & Beholden
Tempered & Turned
Bared & Betrayed

The Shifter Seeker Series:
Raven Rousting (novella)
Coyote Calling (Coming August, 2022)
Holiday Hunting (novella, coming Winter of 2022)
Tiger Tracking (Coming 2023)

Author's Note:

While the Shifter Seeker series can stand alone from the Children of Fenrir series, the events in it occur after that series. So I do recommend reading the Children of Fenrir series first to better orient yourself in the world.

Content Warnings:

The characters go through many trials, and the books are fast paced, often with violence, some killing, and emotional tension. Some characters were emotionally abused as children, some even physically abused. This is not in any way graphic or "on the page" in these novels, but it is part of some of their pasts, and something they continue to deal with the fallout from. Some characters were attacked and bitten in as werewolves. However, there is absolutely no rape, and no dubious sexual consent in these novels.

1

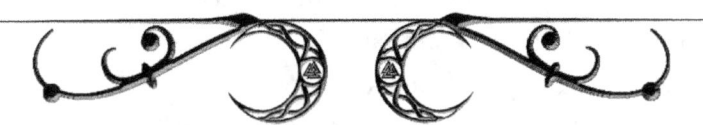

Being the werewolf seeker should have come with a manual, but it didn't. At least, not one I was allowed access to. Since I wasn't a member of one of the packs of Hemlock Hollow, Montana, I couldn't get into their special library filled with the knowledge of thousands of years of history of our kind. Judgy as hell, if one asked me, which they didn't. So, manual-less and irritated, I trudged through the deep February snow of the forest in search of a newly bitten werewolf left on their own to get through the becoming.

My gut told me one was close. They had to be. I only seemed to be able to feel newbies who were on the edge of madness if they were within a mile of me—which sort of felt like a pull deep inside. It was far from an effective locating system. If this really was some sort of Norse God-given ability like so many of my kind thought it was, they needed to work on their power-bestowing details.

No matter which way I went, the pull of the newly bitten didn't get any stronger. But it could be operator error. I wasn't very good at tracking yet. Scents just confused me because now that I was a werewolf there were a million of them, all industrial strength. The snow didn't help matters where that was concerned either. Once upon a time, I'd had a knack for finding things—animals in particular—while hunting with my dad as a kid. Now, not so much. I was literally stumbling around in the dark, tripping over my own tail at times.

Knowing newly bitten would be drawn to the forest, I'd spent the last week visiting every spot of treed land around where I lived in Missoula, Montana. Rough calluses covered my paws from traipsing about in snow-covered granite hillsides. From the limbs overhead, some sort of bird made a weird "crawk" sound at me as if in mocking agreement of my complete and utter failure. I growled my irritation at it, wishing I knew the wolf equivalent of flipping it off. A snick of my teeth in its direction would have to do. That made two things I should have been innately good at that I sucked at—seeking and werewolf speak. I did not exactly have werewolf skills. In my defense, I'd only been one since last summer.

I'd made it through the becoming—or *verða*, as the citizens of Hemlock Hollow referred to it— only thanks to my hot college professor boyfriend, who was irritatingly good at being a werewolf. Then I'd promptly been abducted, had the power of the seeker forcibly awakened in me, called down lightning on accident, and then been manipulated into opening a portal to one of the other nine worlds along with the werewolf reaper and the guy who bit me. Fail, fail, and epic fail.

Through leafless tree limbs with clumps of snow stuck to them, I spied the three-quarter moon and sighed. I had time. As long as I found the newly bitten—or troubled, as I liked to think of them when they were in this state—before the full moon, I could help them so they didn't lose themselves to the madness of instinct and become a mindless killer—or a condemned as the shifter community called them. But each hour that ticked by with no sign of them rang in my head like a death bell. If I didn't find them in time and they didn't overcome the draw of the madness, then my best friend the reaper—a.k.a. Ayra Valdisdöttir—stepped in and put them down.

Heedless of my issues, the horizon had grown a lighter shade of blue. The white blanket of frozen crystals that covered everything made the sky that much more brilliant. Daybreak was almost here, which meant any chance of me finding the troubled tonight was over. I needed food and rest. I'd lost track of them anyways. The snow shower that had rolled through covered any tracks they might have left and totally confused scent trails.

Another loud "crawk" from the limbs above startled me, causing me to brace all four legs out, sinking past my wolf ankles in the snow. I looked up and saw a huge black bird peering down at me, head cocked. A crow, or a raven, maybe. I wasn't exactly up on my birds, so it was anyone's guess. It had the stones to make a guttural sound suspiciously similar to laughter. I growled as I extricated myself from the snow and shook it out from between my toes. To my delight, the bird teetered on the branch and nearly fell, catching itself only because it spread its wings and they snagged in the branches.

Shaking my head, I trotted away. At the edge of the forest I located my weatherproof backpack at the base of the huge fir tree I'd hidden it under. Shifting back to human form with the ease of a thought, I quickly dug the huge beach towel out of my pack and wrapped myself in its fluffiness. Today's snow meant the feeling of wet fur stuck with me.

Towel tucked between my breasts, I pulled my worn jeans on. Actual use had made thin spots through the denim and taken it down to threads in areas. It would have been nice if they were an expensive brand that came that way, but no such luck on the salary of a bartender barely keeping her head above student debt thanks to my attempt at a medical degree I'd likely never finish now. Designer clothes were a guilty pleasure of mine, but they had to take a back burner to food and rent.

A blue flash from my phone told me I had a message. I picked it up and checked. It was from Candice, a newly bitten in young woman I'd helped last summer. We'd become fast friends after I hooked her up with a *verndari*—a person who instructed new werewolves.

Candice: *I need help with something. Can we meet up Wednesday?*

I typed back: *Sure thing. Let me know where and what time.*

To tune out the constant chatter of the clumsy bird, I hummed as I finished dressing, stuffed the towel in my pack, and started out of the forest. The sun was making a spectacular appearance in a pink and purple painted sky when I stepped onto the path leading to the parking lot of the trailhead on the edge of the forest. Two men worked at setting up a camera on a tripod and getting the trailhead just right in the shot. Unfortunately, that put me in the line of sight as well. It was too late to circle around them. My black Jeep sat only three spots from their news van. No doubt they had done that on purpose.

I knew why they were here. It was the same reason I was here—all the animal attacks in the area. And I did not want to talk to them about it. Picking up my pace, I dug my keys out of my jean's pocket. Maybe if I made it before they finished setting up, they wouldn't harass me. One of them spotted me, pointed, and began talking excitedly to the other one about interviewing me. The one with the camera turned it fully in my direction.

Dammit.

"Excuse me, ma'am," the other said as he straightened his peacoat and started my direction.

"You're excused," I mumbled as I stepped off the shoveled path into the snow to go around him. But he followed me quick enough to almost impress a werewolf—certainly quick enough to annoy one.

Brow furrowing, he blinked several times and gaped as if he forgot his next words. I took the opportunity to get a few steps ahead of him without looking supernatural about it. All too quickly, he recovered and dashed to catch up. At this point, I couldn't get away without it being obvious I had inhuman speed. The cameraman grabbed the camera off the tripod and followed at a jog. He slipped a few times on the ice, but recovered quickly with telltale Montana native skill.

"Aren't you worried about the amount of reported wolf attacks in the area?" the reporter asked.

"Nope." I kept walking, stepping back onto the cleared path.

A microphone thrust before me. "Really? Why is that?"

Damn, that had been the wrong thing for me to say. Though I wasn't really sure there was a *right* thing to say with the wolf hating media of this area. I wanted to scream that it wasn't the wolves, not to blame them, not to hunt them down and kill them. But if I did that, it opened up an entirely different can of worms.

"No comment," I said instead.

"But, ma'am, you could be attacked by a wolf. That doesn't frighten you?" he asked, now practically running next to me.

The question made me think of the South Fork wolf pack—just normal wolves—my boyfriend told me had been slaughtered due to supposed attacks. Fury erupted through me in the form of words. "No I couldn't, so no it doesn't." Thankfully I retained the good sense to keep my fangs from extending.

The reporter's eyes lit up. "So you don't believe its wolves behind the attacks. What *do* you think it is?"

Double dammit.

Turning a fierce look on him, I rubbed my flannel covered arms. "I think I'm standing out here in only a flannel and jeans, having cooled down from my hike, and now I'm freezing. So if you'll excuse me."

That flummoxed him so much that he gaped like a fish just long enough for me to spin on my boot heals and march away. I speed walked the remainder of the distance to my rattlecan black Jeep, by no small miracle making it without slipping and falling on my butt. Using just a touch of supernatural speed, I hopped in, shut the door, and cranked the engine to life with the screwdriver in my console. One day when I was out from under the mountain of student debt I'd accumulated on my journey through med school I would get a new ignition switch installed. Right now I was just happy the heater worked like nobody's business. Before one of the news crew could come to my window, or worse get in the way of me backing out, I slammed it in reverse and got out of there.

Disaster averted, I turned my focus to the next one. I had to find a way to figure out these seeker powers of mine before a newly bitten werewolf who needed my help lost their battle with madness before I could make it in time to try and help them. Unfortunately, that meant swallowing my pride, admitting I didn't know what I was doing, and asking for help. Suddenly I wished facing the media was the worst of my problems.

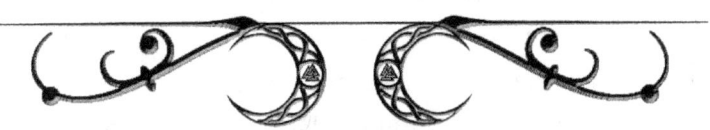

2

When I got to the end of the long driveway leading to Ty's cabin, I found a forest green Wrangler Rubicon 4XE sitting in front of the garage. I pulled up beside it, killed the engine, and got out. Whistling appreciatively, I walked around the fancy looking Jeep. Next to it, my poor old Jeep looked like an ugly duckling. But hey, she was a work in progress. A good long sniff filled my nose with new car smell and…

Excitement filled me. Jogging up the steps onto the front deck of the gorgeous two-story, A-frame style cabin, I called out, "Ayra?" She didn't have a Jeep, but her scent definitely clung to this one. Of course, so did her boyfriend's. As far as I knew, Ty hadn't been expecting a visit from them.

The lavishly tall solid wood front door opened, revealing the reaper of shifterkind. Power radiated from her like heat from a register on full blast. It surrounded her in an aura of swirling shades of purple so dark they were nearly black. Like a mirage, the colors dissipated when I blinked, clearing to reveal the woman within. Waist length, white-blond hair draped over her dainty but muscled left shoulder in a thick braid. Wearing a T-shirt with the name of some Icelandic heavy metal band—which I knew only because I'd asked her once—and black BDUs, she looked ready to go to war. But then, she always looked that way to a degree. The semi-permanent stoic expression she wore only enhanced the look. But I knew a tender, creamy center hid within.

"Hey! You get a new rig?" I asked.

Her braid rose as she gave me a one shoulder shrug. "V did since we had to ditch his truck last summer because of the whole hitting a berserker with it incident."

Only she could make such a statement sound like a casual thing. Berserker's were what the werewolves of Hemlock Hollow called bear shifters. It had been an interesting summer for all of us, to say the least.

She escorted me inside.

The open floor plan allowed us a clear line of sight to the two gorgeous men who sat at the kitchen bar. On the right sat a man with chin-length, wheat blond hair framing robin's egg blue eyes. Just the right amount of muscles filled out his button-up, sapphire shirt. Shades of blue glimmered around him in an aura of power that never failed to take my breath away. His laughing gaze caught mine and he smiled so big crinkles formed at the corners of his eyes. My heart did a huge flutter as my power rose in reaction to his like it always did—Tyler Viðarsson, aka, my hot American-Icelandic professor boyfriend.

Beside him sat a dark-skinned man with close shorn black hair. A T-shirt depicting a comic book Thor stretched tight over his hard chest and hugged his muscled arms to the point of threatening to burst. The shifter power in his aura glowed a gorgeous shade of lavender found in sunsets. He nodded at me and smiled.

"Hey, Sonya."

"Hey, Vidar," I called back. "Nice new ride."

Thirty-two white teeth shone at me—seriously, the man smiled so big and so honestly that I swore I could see all his teeth. It endeared him to me all the more each time he did it.

"She is a beauty, isn't she?" he said with pride.

A groan came from Ayra. "Cars are gender neutral," she said.

We all laughed at that, save for Ayra who I could tell was utterly serious.

Ty rose from the bar and crossed the room to sweep me into his arms and kiss me on the lips. I smacked him lightly on one pectoral when he put me down.

"Ty, we have company," I complained half-heartedly.

He waved a hand. "Ayra and Vidar are not company. They are family."

"True," I agreed, taking a seat at the bar. "But I'm pretty sure they don't want to endure our P.D.A.s."

Shrugging, Ayra sat beside me. "As long as you two don't mate, I'm good."

Heat scorched its way up my neck to my cheeks. "Um, yeah, no I mean. Won't be doing that while you're here."

Much to my relief, Ty eased my pain by going around the bar to the refrigerator and grabbing me a stout. He popped the cap off before handing it to me. "Rough day?" he asked.

"Roughest."

"Still having trouble finding newly bitten?" Vidar asked in a gentle tone.

After a sigh, I admitted, "Yes."

For a long moment, he and Ayra gazed at each other. Then he nodded.

One claw tapped on her chin before Ayra looked over at me. "Vidar's dad has a *völva* he consults with sometimes on cases. She might be able to contact the *vaettir* and see if they have any information, a way to maybe help you find newly bitten *varúlfur*."

"The what and the who?" I knew the term *varúlfur*, it was what the Icelandic descended Hemlock Hollow community called werewolves. The rest of the Americanized Icelandic terms were foreign to me. Though I was attempting to learn Icelandic, many of the terms used by those in

Hemlock Hollow weren't true Icelandic words, only derived from them.

"A *völva* is a practitioner of *seðr*. They are like witches in a way. They can communicate with spirits as well as divine the future."

My mind shattered into a million pieces. "What the actual fuck?" I said for complete lack of a better exclamation, and because, well, my mind had just been blown. Eyes narrowing, my gaze shot to Ty. His mouth gaped as he drew in a breath but struggled to find the words. After a moment of stuttering incoherently, I managed, "Why did no one mention witches and magic were real before now?"

"Your plate's been pretty full. We didn't want to blow your mind any more than it already had been," Ayra said.

I took a long drink of my beer. "That ship has sailed, struck an iceberg, and now lies at the bottom of the Atlantic," I told her. "Shifters, vampires, now witches and spirits. Am I missing anything else?"

Hand covering mine, Ty sat down on my other side. "Most of the creatures of myth and legend are based on fact, and not just those in our own culture."

Several seconds passed in which I gaped stupidly at him and my two other best friends in the world. I had to set my beer down so I didn't either crush it with my werewolf strength or drop it. It shouldn't have surprised me. Before last summer, I hadn't even known werewolves were real. Finally, I found my voice. "So, if I've heard of it, it's probably real?"

Ayra pushed my beer back toward me. "Let's not go down that rabbit hole just yet."

I took another small drink, savoring the complexity of flavors while my brain relaxed enough for me to process more. "Okay, so who is this...*völva*? And please tell me we don't have to go to Iceland to see her."

The room lit up as Vidar smiled. He had a wonderful boyish joy that infused everything around him. Tension eased from me that I hadn't realized I'd been holding on to. I was so grateful he was Ty's best friend, and by proxy, one of mine.

"Her name is Kari Magnusdöttir. She lives outside of Bozeman," Vidar said.

I breathed a sigh of relief. "Good, because I don't have time for a trip halfway across the world right now." Today was Monday and I had to meet Candice on Wednesday. Not to mention, I didn't have the money and I wasn't about to let Ty foot the bill for me. He would in a heartbeat, I had no doubt. But I didn't want him to have to.

As if he knew my thoughts had turned to him, Ty took hold of my hand, his thumb caressing the back of it in a wonderful, maddening way. "Are you sure you are all right with this?" he asked.

Pursing my lips and lifting my shoulders, I told him, "If I'm going deeper into the crazy waters, why not swan dive right off the high jump?"

After three hours in a seat that hugged my backside like memory foam, I had to concede I was glad Ty had offered to drive us in his dark blue Tesla Model Y. I loved my Jeep, but highway driving was definitely not it's thing, and the rigid seats weren't comfortable for much over fifty miles. Plus the grey skies above threatened to open up on us at any given moment and add to the already white landscape. The snow tires on Ty's car combined with the all-wheel drive meant it handled better on the icy roads than my Jeep did.

But the real reason I'd given in was that since buying it last fall, Ty hadn't gotten to drive it much more than to the college where he worked and back. When I'd first been turned into a werewolf last summer his crazy ex-girlfriend blew up his truck in an attempt to scare me—among other things. Turned out what she really wanted was to force Ayra and me to open a portal to the nine Norse worlds. She got her way, but it didn't turn out how she imagined. In the end she had been taken by valkyries to stand trial for her crimes on the planet Muspelheimhr. My mind was still scattered over the whole thing since I'd had no idea any of the Norse stories were real until then.

"Those must be some pretty heavy thoughts," Ty said in a soft voice from the driver's seat.

Just coming out of a slight doze, I made a humming, questioning noise.

"You have not spoke in almost an hour," he pointed out.

I glanced in the rearview mirror at a sleeping Vidar leaning against a window, his jacket tucked up under his head, Ayra sprawled across his lap, sound asleep as well. A smile graced her lips in sleep instead of the usual stoic look she wore. With her white-blond hair splayed out around her she looked utterly peaceful, and nothing like the bad-ass reaper she truly was.

"Thought I'd let them get some rest," I said.

Ty reached over and took my hand in his. The look he gave me said he knew it was more than that. My heart melted. He always seemed to know when I needed comfort. But he had the good sense to let me talk about things in my own time—another thing I loved about him.

"Well, according to the GPS, we are almost there," he said.

My throat suddenly felt too small for my windpipe. I couldn't get enough air.

A gasp came from the back seat. "What happened?" Ayra asked as she sat bolt upright, claws brandished.

"Whoa! Easy on the upholstery, it is new after all," Ty said in a bit of a high voice.

Her gaze shot from Ty, to me, to Vidar, and out each window at the surrounding forest before she relaxed and her claws retracted.

"No one is attacking. We're almost there and I'm just losing my cool a little," I said.

One of her pale brows rose. "I wasn't aware you possessed cool to begin with in regards to this situation."

"In regards to this situation?" I asked.

She hummed a non-committal response and lifted one shoulder. Suddenly awake, Vidar leaned forward and peered at the GPS screen. "Take a left in another mile."

Ty adjusted the screen. "The GPS does not show a road there."

"It's there, trust me."

"Always," Ty replied without hesitation.

Normally their bromance would make me smile. Right now it was all I could do to keep from hyperventilating. Ty's hand tightened around mine and his power flowed over me in a comforting wave. Of its own accord, my own power surged up to meet it. The tension gripping me let up. My throat opened.

"So magic is real," I finally said.

"Yes, in limited amounts in this world, but that's not what Kari does," Vidar said. "She is more like a psychic and a medium than a witch." He thrust his chin toward the windshield. "That's it up ahead."

We turned onto a gravel road hedged in by humongous oak trees that had probably seen the days of prohibition.

"So there are witches?" I asked for clarification.

"In our culture, no. But in others yes. Witches, sorcerers, shamans, they go by many different terms," he said.

"Can anyone be a witch? Cast spells and such?" I asked, relieved at the distraction.

He shook his head. "It's just like being a shifter. You have to be born with the potential in your blood, and they are even more rare than we are. Without teaching, training, nurturing, their abilities won't manifest."

"So no spellcasting for me," I said through a sigh as I leaned my head back against the seat.

Side eyeing me, Ty's lips crooked upward. "Being able to call down lightning is not enough?" he asked.

"Pshh," I turned the noise into a sarcastic sounding puff of air that blew a loose lock of my black hair from my face. "An unpredictable, weather reliant ability that is pretty reckless without Ayra's help," I said.

Ty shrugged.

Storms attracted to me like a magnet, especially when I was upset or scared. Which had been anything *but* a blast when I was a kid. I'd learned to love them over time. A sudden rain storm could chase bullies away, or make me feel like the world cried with me when a boy broke my heart. I'd grown up in northern Washington, which was rainy as a rule anyway, so no one really noticed but me. Until last summer when I'd been changed into a werewolf.

While Ty had helped me through the *verða* we'd discovered I could call down lightning. But it wasn't a cool ability that I could direct anywhere I wanted. It came to *me*, it hit *me*. Which oddly turned out, didn't hurt at all, but instead left me feeling charged and more powerful for a short time. We found out through being manipulated by Ty's ex that I could draw the lightning, and Ayra could direct it, channel it to wherever she wanted it to go. Where Ty's ex wanted it to go was into the guy who'd turned me—her own brother—because he was a "key" that opened a portal to the other nine Norse worlds. It chalked right up there with the craziest summers of my life, topping even the one in Tijuana my freshman year in college.

"Turn at the next left," Vidar said.

In another quarter mile, Ty did as instructed, having to slow down to ease onto the pothole riddled dirt road. We'd left the snow behind fifty miles or so ago. Now we only contended with a thin layer of frost on everything. A mixture of pine and leafless deciduous trees rose up on both sides of the road as if it were the only thing keeping them at bay. Many of the pine trees looked to be at least three feet around, a few even larger than that. We rounded a corner and came upon a cottage tucked between two of the biggest evergreen trees I had ever seen in my life. Redwoods, maybe? I wasn't sure, but their trunks had to be fifty feet around. Each tree trunk was wider than the cottage between them.

To either side of the wooden front door, squat windows sat like squinted eyes. The entire structure appeared to be sided with some type of wooden shingle or shake weathered to gray in most areas. Bushes naked for winter crouched before it, winding around a stepping stone path that led to the door. Vines void of their leaves clung to the corners of the house, rising up to the roof. I imagined in the spring and summer this place would be covered in flowers. Afternoon sun sparkled in the frost that covered absolutely everything, giving the place a magical look that stole my breath.

The Tesla eased to a stop and we piled out into the frigid air.

"Are you certain she cannot do magic?" Ty asked as he took in the place.

Surprised, I turned to him. "You've never met a *völva*?" I asked.

His eyes widened and I almost thought I saw a bit of fear in them for a split second. "I have never had cause to." Yep, there was definitely fear hiding in his voice.

One finger tapping against my leg, I studied him for a moment. This side of him was new to me. "And never wanted to," I observed.

Chest puffing up, gaze going to the cottage, he looked like he might deflect the question, but then he let his breath out. "No I did not. We are not meant to know the future."

Spider legs of fear danced across my skin. I fought back the urge to turn and run from this place. I looked to Vidar. "She isn't going to tell me my future, is she?" I asked.

"No," he assured me quickly. "Not if you don't want her to. Though that's what most people come to *völva* for—well, that or speaking to the spirits—they can do much more than that." He clapped Ty on the shoulder. "They are the keepers of our ways. You may find you have a lot in common with them," he told him.

Ty gave him a tight smile. "Perhaps."

The front door to the cottage opened with a soft creak, drawing our attention. A curvy, middle-aged woman in a pair of black stretch pants and a Caribbean blue tunic leaned against the door frame. Her long, golden hair draped about her in dozens of braids, some French style, some fishbone, others a simple plait. Knotwork tattoos in black and blue wound around her arms.

"Well, are you wolves going to ponder outside my door all day or come in and talk?" she asked though her tone made it sound like she already knew the answer. As if to further prove it, she turned and walked back inside, leaving the door wide open.

Suddenly I really did not want to do this. Magic was one thing, even talking to the dead I could deal with. But someone who could tell the future, *that* I wanted no part of. Considering my complete inability to find newly bitten unless I was within a mile or so of them, though, what choice did I have? Without access to the Hemlock Hollow library, or anyone who knew anything about past seekers—the last of which had died over three hundred years ago—this was currently my best option.

Metaphorically pulling up my big girl panties, I put my shoulders back, chin up, and strode toward the cottage of the *völva*. The first step took me into what I could only describe as a web of power. It felt similar to the charge of a storm, but different, more grounded. It made no sense, but that was how it felt.

"What is that?" I asked, frozen in mid-step.

With a lift of his chin Vidar indicated the surrounding forest. "Part of it's the land. This is a place of power. Part of it's the *völva*. They choose places to live that are conduits of power, so it's often hard to tell one from the other."

Warm, familiar power with the feel of hearth and home wrapped around me like a favorite blanket. Ty stepped beside me and took my hand. "You do not need to be afraid of her. She will not harm you."

The unspoken 'I will not let her' hung between us. He knew I hated to be treated like a damsel in distress and thankfully he had the good sense to hold his tongue. Knowing he wanted to say it, though, I lifted my brows at him.

"I'm not afraid of her." I swallowed my pride and admitted, "I'm afraid of what she might tell us."

Ayra stepped up on my other side. "Nothing she can say changes who you are. And you are a bad-ass," she said in her usual utterly serious monotone.

Laughter bubbled up and surprised me, much like her. I raised my hand and we bumped the sides of our fists together. Through it, her stoic expression never changed, but I felt the humor and support resonating in her power.

Gripping Ty's hand tighter, my reaper best friend and her boyfriend at my side, I strode into the psychic's cottage. The heady scent of dozens of different drying herbs struck me so strong I had to fight back the urge to sneeze. To the right an adorable kitchen decorated in black and white and rooster paraphernalia opened up. Beyond it, soft light poured in from a sunroom where herbs hung from hooks, lines, and lay on a table that looked like it ran the length of the room. In the living room before us a loveseat sat in front of a woodstove where the orange flames of a fire flickered. It all felt very domestic, very normal. Some of my fear drained away.

The *völva's* swinging braids led us into the kitchen where five different colored ceramic cups sat on a butcher block bar. Metal mesh ball tea diffusers hung in them. Vidar must have told her we were coming. She grabbed a steaming copper teapot from the top of a gas stove and poured water into each cup.

Eyes the color of moss looked up and met my gaze. "Please, have a seat." She beckoned to the barstools. "Balder's son has likely already told you my name is Kari Magnusdöttir. But I find it's polite to share introductions. Please call me Kari," she said in a sweet voice with a soothing quality.

As we sat, Vidar introduced us. I met Kari's gaze as I drew the blue teacup closest to me in and wrapped my hands around it. Heat seeped from it into my palms.

Reaching a hand out to cover my cup, Kari met and held my gaze. My skull crawled from the inside, but I had the feeling part of that was my own nerves more than from her digging around in there.

"Do not drink yet." She withdrew her hand. Suspicion almost made me let go of the cup, but curiosity stayed my hands. "You've come to see if there is a way to find the newly bitten who need your help," she said.

Okay, maybe my head *had* been crawling from her digging around in there. Each muscle in my body clenched. Knowing it resonated through my power, and everyone at the table felt it, I focused on the cup in my hands. Slowly, the heat radiating from it soothed me.

As if she were oblivious to my discomfort—which she definitely wasn't, but I appreciated her sparing my pride—Kari went on. "The answer isn't as easy as you might like."

"But there is an answer," I said.

With a nod of her head, she indicated my teacup. "That is the first step. It will open the door to help you discover the answer."

I raised the cup to my nose and sniffed. It smelled earthy and herby, but I couldn't discern one scent from another. "What's in it?"

"In yours? A special mixture, including lavender, mint, peyote, and a few other things," she said through a crooked grin. With a sweep of her gaze, she indicated the other cups. "In theirs, lavender and mint."

I let go of the cup and drew away. "Peyote? What the... Why?" After a few more sputtered attempts at speaking, I rose from the barstool. "You know what, never mind. I don't need to know. And I certainly don't need psychotropics. What I need is answers."

Kari help her hands up in surrender. "My apologies, due to your dual ancestry, there was a chance you'd be open to such methods. The tea will help ease you into the proper state for the ritual necessary to achieve your goals."

Hand going to my hip, I stared her down. Even under intense scrutiny, she didn't flinch and her power didn't falter. "You're serious," I said.

"I am. You're not good at meditation, and meditation is the path along which we must travel," she said.

Grinding my teeth against a retort, I drew a few deep breaths. She wasn't wrong. My mild case of ADHD made meditation almost impossible for me. Add to that being a werewolf who could hear their own blood pulsing through their veins when they went too quiet and it just wasn't going to happen. The fact she knew this about me freaked me out more than a little. I knew without a doubt Ty hadn't told her, and he was the only person who knew I couldn't meditate. Nerves bristling, stomach feeling like I'd just downed a Yaeger bomb, I let out a slow breath.

"I don't like being in an altered state." Which was a nice way of getting around saying I didn't like drugs. The psychologist part of me knew I was avoiding this because of my mother's problems with drugs. I was projecting and deflecting. Still, this was one thing I couldn't get past.

Gaze going distant, Kari tapped her bottom lip with a long, unpainted nail. She took a long drink of her own tea, sighing in satisfaction as she sat the cup down. It made me wonder what was in hers. "There is another way, so long as you have no fear of the dark."

I did *not* like the sound of that. And yet... "I'm listening."

"Deprivation can help achieve the state you need. It means a few hours hike into the mountains."

"No drugs involved?" I checked.

"None whatsoever."

Pushing the offending tea away, I nodded and stood. "I choose option B."

What Kari had left out was that the hike was practically forty-five-degree slope and it ended up being more climbing than hiking. Which wouldn't have been a problem except for the fact we quickly rose into snowy elevations. Thankfully the snow here wasn't nearly as deep as it was in Northern Montana, but even a few inches was enough to make the going tough and slippery as hell. To make matters worse, I seemed to be the only one struggling.

Just when I thought I couldn't go any further, I pulled myself up onto an outcropping and collapsed on the frozen rock to catch my breath. Everyone else sat idly munching protein bars or drinking their water as if they had been waiting for me for hours. It had only been a few minutes, but as casual as they looked, one couldn't tell. Kari leaned back against the rock hillside edging the opening of a deep looking cave, breathing heavy enough to make me feel better about myself. But then she possessed human stamina compared to my werewolf stamina. My one saving grace was that I wasn't tired so much as clumsy when it came to the snow and ice that blanketed much of the landscape.

Ty grasped my hand and helped pull me to my feet. I gave him a smile as thanks. Putting a hand on the small of my back, I stretched, arching to try and ease the ache that had settled there after a particularly nasty slip. Something beneath my hand cracked and suddenly it felt much better. My werewolf constitution kicked in and wiped the remaining ache from my muscles. I enjoyed a good hike as much as the next girl, but when nature added snow and ice, my skills went out the door.

After a few blessed moments of rest, Kari rose. "The rest of you will need to stay here. For this to work Sonya needs to be alone."

Power spiked and Ty gripped my hand a little tighter. "Is it dangerous?" he asked.

"Yes," Kari said without hesitation.

"Then I am going with her," he shot back.

Her eyes narrowed at him. "Then it won't work."

A frustrated growl rumbled in Ty's chest. The wolf in me liked it, a lot. But the woman in me didn't. Using his hand, I pulled him around to face me. "I have to do this. And I don't need a knight in shining armor."

The muscles at the outside corner of his right eye twitched. Guilt dug painful slivers into me. But dammit I was right.

Sighing, Ty looked to Kari. "What does this entail?" he asked.

"She will need to enter a deep meditative state to commune with the Gods, either directly or through a messenger," Kari said.

"That doesn't sound dangerous," Ayra asked, tone suspicious.

Vidar grunted his agreement, arms crossing over his broad chest.

"Her mind will enter a place between worlds. This is dangerous because it separates the mind and body, leaving the body vulnerable to negative forces. But I will be there to protect her from these forces," Kari explained.

"We can protect her body," Ayra said, sounding as if she didn't like this idea any more than Ty did.

Kari shook her head. "She won't be in danger from physical forces, but spiritual ones. It is best you wait here. If I need you, I will call."

My friends exchanged glances in a heavy silence. At last, Vidar clapped a hand on both Ayra and Ty's shoulders, but met my gaze. "We can trust her. If she says this is how it has to be done, I believe her."

I nodded my thanks to him. "V's right. I got this. No worries, guys. If I need you, I will holler," I said.

Ty pulled me in against him, his free hand going around behind my back. His full, soft lips settled over mine in a gentle touch that almost felt reverent. As he drew away, he breathed into my partially opened mouth, "Be safe," in the barest of whispers.

I smiled wider, now tingling all the way down to my toes. "Always."

After a moment of mustering up my willpower, I let go of his hand and took a step toward the gaping mouth of the cave. It suddenly looked very deep and very dark. The troubled newly bitten needed my help. And if I was to help them, I needed to know how to do what I was meant to do.

"Let's do this," I said to Kari.

She inclined her head and led the way into the pitch black unknown.

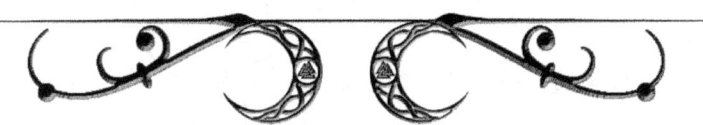

3

Disappointment shot through me when Kari pulled a tiny flashlight from her pocket and turned it on. It wasn't that I minded her using one—myself, I could see fine in the dark thanks to my werewolf eyesight. Part of me had been hoping she might utter a spell for light, or use a magical item, or something. Sure, Vidar had said *völva's* didn't use magic, but I'd still been somewhat hopeful.

The cave turned into a yawning cavern that dipped down at a somewhat steep angle. Walls of white granite speckled with black lichen reflected the soft beam of the flashlight. Each step I took I felt a tug on the threads of my power woven with Ty's, and even Ayra's and Vidar's. It felt like a lifeline, or a rappel line held by a spotter. The sensation eased my anxiety slightly.

"What is this place?" I whispered as we descended.

Kari smiled like a proud mother, her gaze not on me, but the walls of the cavern. "A place of power."

"Vidar said that about your cottage."

"This entire area is a place of power, but here, it is concentrated by a conduit."

Prickles of dread tap danced across my skin like fairies wearing stilettos. That thought made me wonder if fairies were real too. I was *so* not ready to ask.

The cavern veered sharply to the left and kept going down at an angle steep enough to make me lean back. With each step power grew thicker in the air. It felt similar to what I'd felt back at Kari's home, only denser, stronger. I didn't like the idea of going so far underground. Being away from the open sky and access to lightning—my best defense—made me nervous. I had to keep my mind busy.

"You knew I'd turn down the tea." Being psychic, I figured the likelihood was high, but I knew so little about her kind that I couldn't be sure.

"It was likely," she answered, the lilting tone of her voice suggesting there was more to it.

"Then why bother offering it?"

The flashlight messed up my werewolf night sight making it so I couldn't see her expression.

"There was a small chance you would have accepted it."

Her tone told me what I needed to know. "And you preferred that method to whatever it is we are about to do."

"Yes."

"Why?"

It took her a little longer to answer this time. "This way is more…immersive, more direct."

"And more dangerous," I guessed.

Suddenly the cavern leveled out and opened up. My next stride felt like stepping off an airplane into an Alabama airport in the middle of summer—air so thick it resisted anything passing through it. Kari switched off her flashlight. In another breath my eyesight adjusted. Hundreds of glowing green crystals covered the high roof and cascaded down the walls like falling stars. A huge round pool of softly glowing Caribbean green water dominated the floor of the cavern. Steps had been carved into the stone leading into it. Steam billowed from the water.

"Oh my Gods. This place is beautiful," I whispered out of respect for the utter serenity of the room. Despite the density of the power literally throbbing in the place, it felt welcoming, invigorating.

As we grew closer, I realized Norse runes had been chiseled into the stone in a circle around the pool. I bent down to touch one and could have sworn the air about it shimmered like the desert on a hot summer day. More than that, it sparkled. Though I recognized the runes as Elder Futhark, the more ancient version, I couldn't quite read it. "What does it say?" I asked.

Kari stopped by the wall. I realized only when she took her backpack off and sat, that a stone bench stretched for several feet along the wall. "It is an old poem. The meaning translates to, 'Come all those who wander, rest your battle-weary bones and ponder', basically."

"So this is a place of rest?"

She inclined her head toward the pool. "This place, yes. Where we're going, no."

Starting to wonder about her, I took a closer look around the room, but I didn't see another exit. "Um, is there a hidden door or something?" I really, really hoped she wasn't about to say something about swimming to our destination. I liked the water, but swimming underwater in a cavern sounded far too much like a scene from a horror movie. While I was a fan of horror movies, I was *not* a fan of acting them out.

"No," she said. She took a pair of metal travel cups from her pack, a clear wine bottle filled with some kind of golden hued liquid, and two large towels. "And no, we don't have to swim to our destination."

Of course she knew I was about to ask that. "You let me ask most of the questions I ask to make me feel better," I observed.

Grinning, she set her items down beside the steps leading into the pool. "It makes people uncomfortable when they realize I know most of what they're going to say."

"Most?"

"Every choice people make changes things. The future is not set in stone. Being psychic is far from an exact thing, and it is different for each *völva*," she explained.

She began untying her shoes, so I followed suit. "How so?"

"Some see glimpses of possible futures down one path, some see all paths. Others require a conduit like rune stones or tarot cards. Some can see only moments into the future, some years, or even lifetimes. And there are psychics outside of our culture who see in completely different ways."

Part of me wanted to ask how she saw, and how much, but a bigger part of me was too afraid to know. Did my future involve Ty, maybe a family with him? Would Ayra and Vidar be there? Or would Ragnarök come about because of us? I let out a long breath. Some things one was better not knowing. The psychologist in me knew if I did know the second guessing would be endless.

"So where are we going?" I asked instead. Into the pool, obviously, since Kari unzipped her jeans and began to shimmy out of them. But I had a feeling it involved more than just that.

"The astral plane, where we will hopefully find a conduit of the Gods, or maybe even a seeker of old."

Hearing the words made me wonder if nothing could surprise me anymore. "Is that like the spirit realm?"

"No. Everything in the astral plane is made up of energy. We will enter it in our energy forms."

"But we can find past seekers there?"

"Yes. I've come across them on several occasions."

Everything I'd read or been taught said the dead went somewhere, but the astral plane had never come up. "They don't move on to the Elysian fields, or Valhalla, or heaven, or…I don't know, somewhere more permanent?"

"They do. But since spirits are energy, they can still travel to the astral plane if they haven't moved on to another life."

Blowing out a breath, I shook my head. This information piled atop the stack of things I would have to process more fully at a later time.

Kari folded her jeans neatly, then pulled her T-shirt off, did the same, and laid it atop the jeans. Her bra and panties followed. Gaze going back to the pool, I suddenly put things together.

"Sensory deprivation, ah, I see."

Determination overrode my unease and I stripped down as well, my clothes ending up in a far less neat pile. My hands hesitated at the necklace I always wore, the one Ty had given me for Yule.

Fingers tracing the crescent moon and raven sitting on it, both formed of knotwork, I tried to gather my courage. This all felt so foreign. It made me not want to part with my touchstone.

"You can leave it on. It will help tether you," Kari said.

"Tether?"

"Your energy, your spirit, will be traveling, not your body. The necklace is sentimental to you, therefore it is a tether that is both physical and power."

Though a late February chill permeated the cavern, heat radiated off the pool. That combined with my werewolf constitution kept me just above chilly. Still, the water invited me, little fingers of steam reaching out to wrap around my toes.

"Go ahead and get in. Find a place that feels comfortable to you," she said.

I did as instructed, walking into spring water that easily rivaled the hottest spa tub I'd ever been in. Some part of me had expected it to feel slimy. Instead it felt like the clean spring water. On top of that, it smelled amazing—like a snowmelt river with mint growing along its banks. The water level came nearly to my waist. Along the edge, I found a bench hewn directly from the granite. When I sat the water came just under my chin. Its warmth enveloped my body and both the weariness of the hike, and a good amount of stress, seeped from me.

"So how's this work?" I asked, my voice already slow and relaxed.

Covered by only her multiple long, blond braids, Kari walked to the other side of the room where a stone bowl sat tucked into a cubby carved into the wall. I hadn't even noticed it until she reached in. She picked up the bowl and carried it back to the pool.

"I will put up a circle to protect our bodies and help keep the way unobstructed for our return. Then we will go into a meditative state and project our energy bodies into the astral plane. Once there we will travel to the place seekers of old frequent," she explained.

"Oh, that's all."

After a brief smile at my flippancy, her eyes went all distant and she reached into the bowl. Power pulsed around her. I got the distinct impression the time for questions had ended.

"Hail, Frigg, we beseech you to empower our astral bodies for travel," she began in a rhythmic chant. With each word, her power increased, and with each word, she sprinkled a handful of the stuff from the bowl along the outside of the circle of runes. Salt, I realized.

"Hail, Odin, we beseech you to guide us to the answers we seek."

The resonation of the words through the chamber had a calming effect that soon made my eyes droop.

"Hail, Sif, we beseech you to guide us safely through a foreign land."

I realized at the mention of each of the gods, she stopped at a cardinal point along the circle of water—north, east, south.

"Hail, Thor, we beseech you to imbibe us with strength to fight our opposers."

Up until that last one, I'd been growing calmer, feeling lighter. But now I wondered once again about the danger of our undertaking. Why could nothing in this brave new world I'd been plunged into be easy?

At the last words, Kari sprinkled a final bit of salt to close the circle, then she stepped down into the pool. Turning, she picked up the wine bottle and popped the cork out with her teeth. She poured some into each of the two cups, then waded through the water to hand me one. Not sure if I should speak yet, I lifted my brows and looked from her to the cup.

Still in that chanting tone, she answered my unspoken question. "We drink of this mead to honor and thank the gods, and to bless us on our journey."

I accepted the cup and lifted it to my lips. The strong, delicious scents of honey alcohol and spices drifted to me. Having been a bartender for much of my adult life as I worked my way through college, I knew the scent of mead well enough. As Kari tipped it back, so did I. The taste of sunshine and summer spilled across my tongue and I swallowed it readily. Before I knew it, I downed the entire cup. But then, so did she. The warmth of the alcohol spread through me and reached out. As it did, I felt as though I became one with the water, like my body ceased to exist. Weightlessness set me adrift. My mind lazily pondered whether or not I'd tasted any drugs in the mead. But I hadn't. That left only one other option: Kari possessed at least a little magic. Though it might just be brewing the strongest mead known to this planet, regardless, it was still magic in my opinion.

"Imagine a body of energy hovering above you, one identical to your physical body," Kari said in a low, soothing tone.

I did as instructed, imagining looking into a mirror to get the image right.

"Now allow your spirit to float up and settle into it," Kari continued. Something compelling in her tone helped me become weightless and float upward into the body of energy I'd created.

The cavern ceiling swelled toward us, the glowing green crystals in it becoming brighter, larger. No, not larger...closer. So close I could touch them, only my hand didn't look like flesh and bone any more, not exactly. It still held the shape of my hand, down to the creases over my fingers. But my coloring was wrong, too bright and soft at the same time, as if I were made of energy. Recalling what Kari had said about that, I turned to look at her—and found myself looking down on the pool from twenty feet up.

My body lounged beneath me in the pool. Head resting against the stone edge, my black hair floated around me like a dark cloak, breasts floating almost high enough to break the surface of the teal water. I looked peaceful, something I hadn't felt in a long time. Across from my body sat Kari's, her eyes closed and head back as well. Prickles of unease, of…otherness, started to work through me.

"Easy. You are safe. Relax. If you get too stressed, your cord will pull you back into your body," came Kari's calming voice from right next to me.

I looked over—not my body, but my astral self—at her floating in the air next to me close to the ceiling. She glowed the most beautiful lavender and white I'd ever seen.

"Cord?" I asked.

She nodded and pointed to my astral body's abdomen. Sure enough, an energy cord of sorts extended from where my belly button would be if I were flesh, all the way down to the abdomen of my physical body. Cord wasn't quite accurate, though. It looked more like a beam of bluish energy.

"Whoa," I said.

"It probably won't, but if anything approaches us, remember to protect that cord."

"Why?" I asked.

"It's how you get back to your body." Smiling, she beckoned with a hand. "Come."

And so we rose into the mystic.

4

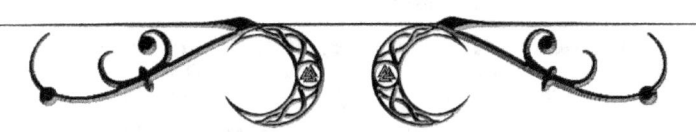

Propelled by power, will, I had no idea, Kari began to ascend through the ceiling. I thought about following and suddenly began to rise—directly into the solid rock of the cave ceiling. Kari's lavender-hued form rose alongside me, giving me a knowing smile. No sense of pressure, or entrapment came like I expected. I simply rose. The rock felt like the consistency of pudding that had been in the refrigerator over night, only warm and inviting. So much power lay in the granite that it left me breathless.

Before I could contemplate the meaning of that, we were through it. The entire world looked different, and yet the same in shape and general appearance. Everything glowed with what I could only describe as life. Trees, grass, and bushes emanated soft variations of green from beneath their snow cover, bare rock glowed grey, and animals exuded many different colors. Part of me longed to descend and touch things to see if they felt different. They definitely smelled different, fresher, more vivid and alive. How I could smell without a physical nose was beyond me.

Just like on our plane, bird song filled the air, but unlike our plane it had a symphony sound to it, harmonic and coordinated.

"Come," Kari called, reminding me our visit here had a purpose.

We rose above the forest and began to soar across the open sky. The wind caressed my being, not quite rolling off, but not going through me either. It tickled and invigorated me at the same time. Arms out like wings, I laughed. Kari laughed with me, the same joy I felt reflected back at me from her face. With a tilt of her shoulder, she dipped and flew closer to me.

"The next part is where it gets a bit prickly, so we'll need to keep quiet as possible," she said.

Afraid to answer, I nodded. I wasn't sure how much good keeping quiet would do when we lit up the sky like two lavender and blue stars. But not knowing what odd sorts of danger might lurk in this place, I wasn't going to chance it.

She began to draw away from me. Much like shifting forms, I simply thought about going faster, and I did. Soon we streamed across the afternoon sky—which I now noticed held no sun. Our pace would have pulled tears from my eyes had I possessed a body. Also unique to this form, I felt no resistance from the wind. It parted easily, almost as if we were akin to it, part of it in a way. The sensation was so odd my mind couldn't quite grasp it. Before I knew it, the landscape beneath us changed from forest to high desert, then to rolling planes, then to swamplands. The light changed as well, as if the day progressed more with each new landscape we flew over.

One strange thing stood out—there were no cities, no houses, no buildings or evidence of civilization of any sort, that I was used to, at least. Just as I began to contemplate this, the land disappeared and we were soaring over the glowing blue ocean at night. Above us a canopy of stars glowed with more colors than I thought possible. Amidst them swirled the hues of what may have been nebulas, and maybe even other galaxies.

"What the…?" The words escaped me as the barest whisper.

Kari began to slow down.

Islands appeared ahead in the vast water. We passed a rather large one and slowed even more. With only a thought about slowing down, my astral body responded. Strangely, it felt utterly natural. Something about the place we descended to felt familiar, like I should know it. At the edge of a long beach palm trees swayed, casting off their soft green and yellow glow as if painting the air about them. Countless points of light in all different colors glowing in the ocean drew my attention. The body of water literally teamed with the lights. My instinct knew what they were without a closer look—the astral bodies of animals. Unfortunately, the oceans of earth no longer held this much life. Sadness filled me without the sting of tears. But then, I had no physical body, so I supposed I couldn't actually cry.

I was so caught up in my thoughts and the sights, that I didn't realize Kari was leading us to the beach until we were settling onto it.

Sand warmed my energy feet. While I couldn't exactly feel the grittiness between my toes, I could feel the life that radiated from the billions of ground down shells that made up the beach. The sensation felt so odd that I was compelled to bend down and reach for a handful of sand. Despite not having a physical body, I was still able to pick it up and let it run through my fingers.

Kari touched my arm, stirring me from my musings. I looked over and found her giving me a knowing smile.

"It never gets old," she said softly.

"Where are we?" I whispered.

She gave me a sly look. "Tortuga, well, Tortuga in the astral realm."

What the... "No way." My words were quiet enough a werewolf would have had trouble hearing them. Kari could have knocked me over with a feather—quite literally, I was sure, considering my astral form. We had traveled across the entire United States and further in mere minutes. That big island we'd passed must have been Cuba.

With a tilt of her head, she beckoned for me to follow her. We left the beach and went into the cover of the palm trees. Up and up we climbed, going deep into a jungle the likes of which I had never seen, and never would see on our plane. I was so busy gawking at the glowing fauna that I nearly missed the cliff edge Kari stopped at. My proverbial heart leaped into my proverbial throat as my toes gripped the grassy edge. Managing to float backward toward safer ground, I remembered I could fly and suddenly felt very foolish.

To our left between two palm trees clinging to the edge of the cliff, swung a hammock. Someone lounged in it, legs hanging out the sides. Their form glowed a mixture of blue and green. That energy, that power... Something deep inside me responded to it, recognized it.

"*Leitar*," I whispered. I had no idea why the Icelandic term for seeker came out of my mouth, but it just felt natural in this instance.

The person in the hammock sat up so abruptly they nearly tumbled out of it. Beneath the blue-green glow of energy was a tall woman of muscular build with a thick braid of wheat blond hair draped over her shoulder nearly reaching her waist. She wore a dark blue blouse cinched beneath a brown leather corset that looked like it doubled as armor. Black breeches disappeared into knee-high black leather boots. The look was downright...pirate-like. Even on her astral body I saw a hint of four vicious scars cutting along the edge of her right cheek, jaw, and neck.

"Whoa." Shock stole any intelligent response I had, leaving me with only that.

In reply, she said something in a language I didn't know. The next words she spoke had the inflection of a question and ended in a word that sounded something like "Dutch".

I shook my head. "I'm sorry. I don't speak Dutch, if that's what you're asking." Concerned, I turned to Kari.

Bottom lip pulled between her teeth, she looked at me with wide eyes. "I didn't anticipate this. I've only seen her once before, and I didn't try to speak to her. When on the astral plane it's best to avoid talking to other beings unless necessary."

The rumblings of a growl started in my chest, but I squashed it. This wasn't her fault. She brought me this far, which was much farther than I could have come on my own. Now it was up to me.

I looked back to the pirate seeker and tapped my chest. "Sonya." Head cocked, I pointed to her.

Smiling, she said, "Lucretia."

Encouraged by the progress, I asked, "Do you speak English?"

She pushed off the hammock and literally walked on air until her feet touched down on the grass next to me. "Little. Yes."

"Thank Thor," I uttered beneath my breath.

At that she smiled, the motion pulling at the scar on her check, but not detracting one bit from her fierce beauty. For her astral body to do it, the move had to be old muscle memory etched deep into her psyche. At least, the psychologist in me figured that had to be how it worked. Green eyes filled with curiosity, she walked around me, looking from my head to my hiking boots. In a T-shirt, flannel, and jeans I had to look very strange to her. I also realized our astral bodies must project the image of what we'd last worn. Interesting. I'd be psycho analyzing this experience for a long time to come.

Another much more disturbing thought occurred to me. "Why are you here?" Why hadn't she moved on? Why wasn't she at peace somewhere, or off starting a new life, whatever came after? Surely this plane wasn't all there was.

"Waiting for you."

That opened up a whole new can of worms, but with our language barrier, I couldn't ask her a million questions. So I settled on, "Why?"

"*Gids ritueel*," she said.

Not understanding, I shook my head and shrugged.

"Help seek..." Brows scrunching together, she waved a hand in the air as if trying to catch the word. "...*verontrust*."

Relief mixed with concern. Did every previous seeker have to wait here for the next? I had to at least try to ask. "Have you been waiting here all this time?"

She tapped her chest, and I had a feeling she indicated not herself, but her heart, or maybe her power. "Knew when."

That was comforting, sort of. "Good. I wouldn't want you stuck here because of me."

Head cocked, she took a moment, obviously trying to process my words. With a beckoning gesture, she walked away from the cliff. I followed. She stopped in a small area free of trees or underbrush.

"Must hurry. Will bring *Jötnar*."

Spikes of anxiety shot through me. I looked to Kari—who had stayed put next to one of the palm trees by the cliff. The look of alarm on her face did not bring me comfort. "I feared something like that might happen," she said.

From the legends my dad told me as a child I knew the *Jötnar*—frost giants—were from *Jötunheimr* and weren't exactly friendly with the Aesir, who I was supposedly chosen by.

Head thrown back, gaze on the sky, Lucretia spread her arms wide and began to chant. Though I had no idea what she said, I could tell by the reverent look on her face she was probably talking to the gods. Her voice took on a rhythm. After several verses that flowed easily off her tongue, she paused and thunder boomed overhead. Clouds had rolled in, odd looking things that glowed a muted off-white.

Lucretia's hand touched mine and I looked down to find her directly before me. Wickedly long claws adorned her fingers. Gaze fixed to mine, she turned my hand over, palm up.

"Blood sacrifice to gods. Small. Opens the way," she said.

I didn't like the sound of that on so many levels. But I knew enough about the Norse ways to know this requirement wasn't unusual. And yet allowing a stranger to cut me fell way out of my comfort zone. For a long moment I just stared at her. Eyes the color of Caribbean seas held my gaze with unflinching confidence. Her power flared like hearth and home, like kinship. This woman was no stranger. She was my seeker sister. I nodded.

One of Lucretia's razor sharp claws sliced a long line across my palm. But no blood came because I had no skin for her claw to break. Instead, my astral body gave way like gelatin. A mixture of blue and gold energy began to leak from the opening like mist. Pain lanced into me much like it can when one knows they've been cut but can't feel it until they see the blood. Lucretia began chanting in a foreign language again. Power flared from her, jumping to me. My own pulsed and met it, holding it at bay out of sheer instinct. I breathed out. My walls dropped. Warmth spread from my hand, up my arm, and throughout my body.

Still chanting, Lucretia cut her own palm, then clapped our hands together. At the moment our astral bodies touched, lightning lit up the sky. I looked up in time to see it shoot straight for us. Then all became bright white.

I'd been hit by lightning many times. It was a seeker thing. But this felt different. Normally it energized me, made me feel like I could take on the world. This felt more like the lightning opened a door inside me. Or maybe it was more like *I* opened to something. When the bright white faded, I felt not only energized, but awake in a way I'd never been before.

Lucretia wore the same huge grin I felt on my own face. "Is done," she said.

I opened my mouth to ask her what exactly "it" was, when the ground shook beneath our feet—not literally, but more like its energy pulsed. Regardless of the oddity of the sensation, I knew what it meant. Something was coming.

Drawing a glowing white scimitar I would have sworn hadn't been across her back a moment ago, Lucretia smiled as she looked to the horizon. That expression proved we had less in common than I originally thought.

"Go. I give you time," she said.

From the feel of the power approaching, I got the very distinct impression it wasn't just one *Jötnar*, not by a long shot. "No. I'm not leaving you to fight them alone."

She turned that smile on me and I saw pure joy in it. "*Ja*. Is time," she insisted.

"Time? For what?" I asked.

"Valhalla."

Panic edged in. "No!" I couldn't let her sacrifice herself for me.

But she wasn't listening. She had turned her back and started marching into the jungle. I moved to go after her, but Kari grabbed my arm and stopped me. Her wide eyes bore into me.

"You musn't. We have to go," she said. Her energy wrapped around my arm in a way her fingers couldn't and tugged harder.

"I can't leave her to die," I protested as I watched Lucretia's bouncing braid disappear into the jungle.

"Sonya." The urgency in Kari's voice made me turn to look at her. "Lucretia died three hundred years ago. This is her spirit visiting the astral plane to meet you. She has no body waiting for her like we do. If she dies here, she will move on and she is long overdue for that."

Spirts, different planes, it was a bit much for my analytical brain. It wasn't that I didn't believe in it. How could I not, considering I literally stood on another plane at the moment? It was just too much to process all at once, like trying to figure out the logistics of time travel. Gods, I hoped that wasn't a thing. I gave in to Kari's pull.

One small tug launched us into the sky. We became weightless. The ground fell away and began to pass beneath us at a blinding speed. Jungle green blurred into ocean blue. Pressure built in the air behind us, hot and menacing. I glanced back. Four human shapes flew after us. Though they were far enough away to be nearly against the horizon, the fact I could make out their silhouettes spoke of how large they were. Dark storm clouds roiled overhead, creating a dramatic background against which the pursuers astral bodies glowed brilliant blues and greens. I couldn't make out anything other than that about them. Part of me wanted to. I'd never seen a *Jötnar*. But the smart part of me knew that if I got to see these particular *Jötnar* up close, it would be the last thing I saw.

I pushed myself faster until Kari no longer pulled on my arm, but instead had to increase her own pace. The green land beneath us turned to golden fields. The pressure behind us increased at the *Jötnar* grew closer. Glancing over my shoulder,

I saw they had closed half the distance between us. They weren't big and blue like I expected, tall, yes, and muscular like nobody's business, but pale skinned. The long hair streaming out behind them may have been blue, but it might also have just been skewed by the glow of their astral bodies. In their hands they held very sharp, very big, swords.

Panic dug its massive claws deep into me. It helped me find an entirely new gear of speed. Scrubby desert flew by beneath us, then finally, mountains. We slowed abruptly and started to descend. The moment we did, though, they were upon us. Their energy reached us first. It hit us like the pressure before a storm, only with a physical impact that knocked us both to the ground. I hadn't even made it to my feet before they landed all around. Power rolled off them like a sonic wave, striking and pinning us. It felt somewhat like how I imagined being hit by a linebacker would feel.

Pissed and more than a little scared, I forced myself to rise to my feet.

The sensation of not being able to breathe swept over me as I looked up, and up, realizing how incredibly tall these beings were—at least seven feet. They didn't threaten or exchange witty banter with us. Swords and battle axes flashed as they attacked in a flurry of glowing limbs and hair. They swung for the cord of energy leading from my belly to the ground. I only had time to suck in a breath to scream before Kari grabbed my arm and pulled me down.

I fell, not to the ground, but *through* it.

Oh yeah, astral plane. In my panic, I'd somehow forgotten that. Panic surged again as I fell, and fell, and didn't stop.

The feeling of falling turned abruptly to an odd suction sort of sensation. I hit bottom—the bottom of what, I had no idea at first. Everything felt heavy. Then I realized that was because I was back in my body, my flesh and blood one. The scream I hadn't got to release flew from my lips, followed by all the colorful curses I knew in Swedish and several I'd recently picked up in Icelandic. Water splashed as I spun to look all around me, more than half expecting our pursuers to have followed us. But no one was in either the cave or the pool besides Kari and me.

Across from me, Kari rose. A hot blush colored her cheeks. Whether it was from the warm water, or our flight from the *Jötnar*, I couldn't tell. Her hands shook visibly as she walked up the stone steps, grabbed one of the towels, and wrapped herself in it. Seconds after she did, the slap of rapid footsteps sounded in the cavern beyond. In another heartbeat, I was out of the pool. Water sloshed, washing away some of the salt.

"Oh no!" I bent to try and fix it, but Kari stopped me with a hand on my arm.

"It's okay. We're safe now," she assured me.

I accepted the towel she held out and wrapped it around myself. Though I didn't completely doubt her, I didn't want to face my doom naked either in case she was wrong. I found lifting my arms took some effort. My body felt so heavy after the weightlessness of the astral plane.

Ty, Ayra, and Vidar burst into the cave looking ready for battle. I didn't blame them. My own energy still buzzed just beneath my skin in preparation. Blue eyes wide and wild with worry, Ty scanned my naked body before glancing around the room.

"I'm okay. We're okay," I assured him before he could ask.

"Then why the screaming?" Ayra asked, claws out, gaze scanning the cave as if she wasn't quite convinced of our safety.

Humming to buy time, I contemplated what exactly to reveal. If I said too much they would worry, and that would lead to them not wanting me to do things on my own in the future.

"*Jötnar* chased us back here," Kari spilled the beans.

"What?" Ty and Ayra exclaimed at the same time.

"So cool," Vidar whispered.

Ayra smacked him on his bulging right biceps hard enough to echo through the cave.

I glared at Kari. "That is over dramatizing the situation a wee bit," I said with a forced smile.

Lips pinching together, nose pulling down, she looked up at a random spot on the ceiling. "No. That is adequate dramatization."

Groaning, I dropped my head into my hand— the one not holding the towel closed. Suddenly Ty stood before me, his hands on my shoulders. "You are not hurt are you?"

The urge to be angry at his overprotectiveness rose, but looking into his scared baby blues, I couldn't bring myself to.

"I'm fine. We got back before they could attack, thanks to Kari's quick thinking," I said, shooting her a smile. She returned it and inclined her head slightly.

"Are we in any danger now?" Ayra asked.

Kari let out a long breath. "No. Astral bodies can't cross into this plane without their physical body waiting here for them."

A delighted noise came from Vidar. "*Jötnar!* That is amazing. What did they look like? Do they have blue skin? Why did they attack you?" he asked, filled with boyish excitement.

Such enthusiasm made me laugh, releasing some of the tension that gripped me. "I'll tell you all about it on the ride home. I'm starved and pretty sure I'm headed for an adrenalin crash."

With a nod, Ty retrieved the bundle of my clothes from the stone bench. "Did you at least find your answers?" he asked.

Grabbing my T-shirt from the bundle and pulling it on, I thought about his question. "I'm not entirely sure. But I found...something."

The ritual the pirate seeker and I had started *was* something. Of that I had no doubt. But had we finished it? I took a moment to reach inside and touch my power. It did feel a bit different, almost as if it's resonation had been slightly altered, like a tuning fork being struck. Odd. What that meant, I had no idea.

5

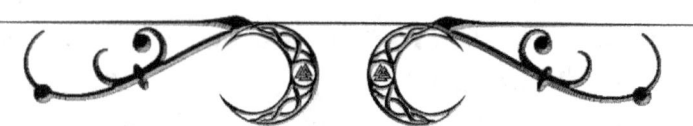

The loud beep of my alarm app cut through a very disturbing dream about sword wielding blue giants from another planet. Regardless, I fought the impulse to snatch the phone off the bedside table and throw it across the room. I'd gladly take on a few *Jötnar* for another half hour of sleep after the double shift at the bar I'd just pulled.

It took a moment to realize the tone wasn't my alarm, but my notification for texts. Groaning, I extricated an arm from the blankets and groped around until my fingers found my phone. The cool air outside my cocoon made me utter a few colorful words. Sure, as a werewolf I was highly tolerant of cold, but when I slept I liked to be warm and toasty. And it didn't help that I couldn't afford to run the wall heaters in my cheap apartment with its barely-there insulation and building code breaking 2x4 walls. I pulled the phone back under the blankets with me.

Candice: *Sorry. I know it's a day early. But I'm kinda freaking out. Can we meet now?*

I sat bolt upright, chilly room and lack of sleep forgotten. I typed out a quick response.

Me: *Of course. Name the place. I can come now.*

Candice: *Coffee shop on Broadway. I'm there now.*

That was only a few minutes from my apartment on the edge of town. I glanced at the clock on my bedside table. It was nearly noon.

Me: *Be there in ten.*

Throwing the covers aside, I shot from my bed. With werewolf speed, it took less than two minutes to get dressed, run a brush through my hair, and pee. Slowing it down for any humans who might be outside, I grabbed my keys and dashed down the rickety metal stairs hugging the side of the brick building. My flat black Jeep waited in my designated parking spot below. Due to the snow, I'd put the top back on, mostly for appearances sake. I loved the wind in my hair as much as any canine, but people cast weird looks and asked a lot of questions when I drove around in a topless Jeep and the average high temp for the month was in the forties.

I hopped in, fired her up, and took off, checking my speed when the tires chirped as I shifted into third gear. Few, if any, would notice in my shady neighborhood, but I didn't like to take chances. The cops didn't even frequent this part of town. Not that they were afraid to, it wasn't all that bad. The city just didn't have the budget to hire enough cops anymore—much like everywhere else in the world. Safety was slowly falling out of fashion with voters who could barely afford the price of milk or gas. Still, I tried to keep my speed reasonable. My foot ached to depress the accelerator. Candice had sounded so desperate. True, a person couldn't really sound anyway in a text, but she generally down played how bad things were, not the opposite.

Could it be something to do with her *verndari* in Hemlock Hollow? Or the werewolf family she was staying with there? I had hoped the family might like her, she'd like them, and she'd want to stay.

When I'd found Candice she hadn't shifted yet, which meant she hadn't gotten through the *verða*. But I'd been a newly bitten myself at the time and had been totally incapable of helping her through it, so Ty had hooked her up with a *verndari* in Hemlock Hollow, and a host family. While there she was finishing her senior year of high school as well.

At the last moment, I processed the red light ahead of me and hit the brakes. The tires left rubber on the asphalt, but I managed to stop in time. Thankfully, no one was behind me, so I didn't get rear ended.

"Dammit!"

As the cycle of the light cooled my anxiety, I took a few deep, cleansing breathes—the kind Ty was always trying to teach me about during our meditation sessions. He had started out as my *verndari* before we became much more, and still helped me with all things wolfy. Right now he was off being an amazing history professor at U of M, so I'd just have to channel his lessons. For Candice's sake, I managed to pull myself together. She was the first newly bitten I'd helped, and pretty much entirely by accident, so the last thing I wanted to do was fail her now.

Finally, I pulled into the coffee shop parking lot. I spotted Candice sitting on a bench beneath a fir tree, the evergreen boughs spread over her like an umbrella, casting her in shadow. Something about it gave me a chill and made me jump out of the Jeep all the faster. Brown hair with its signature purple streak twisted up into a clip that made it stick out in every direction, and a wrinkled black T-shirt with a faded grey pi symbol on it made her look like a college student recovering from an all-nighter. Black BDU pants and black platform combat boots completed the look. The way she clutched the paper coffee cup in her hand like a lifeline coupled with her constantly roving eyes gave an entirely different impression though.

The real tell might have been the way her power popped like pitchy firewood. Pungent fear wafted from her, carrying all the way across the parking lot to me. Shoving my hands in the pockets of my jean jacket, I crossed over to her at a clipped pace. I'd only made it a few steps from the Jeep before her gaze locked onto mine. The desperation written all over her face coupled with the way every muscle in her body seemed to tense at once, made it clear she wanted to leap up and run to me. In a few more steps, I reached her and sat down.

"What's up? They're treating you okay in Hemlock Hollow, aren't they?" I asked.

She blew air out through her lips, making the strand of purple hair that had escaped her clip move from her face. "They're controlling tools. But that isn't the issue."

I locked my teeth against a reply, but I made a mental note to return to the subject. "What is?"

Sighing in a dramatic way that made her seem younger than her eighteen years, she clutched her coffee cup tighter. "I made friends with another newly bitten in Hemlock Hollow, Fernando Ruiz. He got tired of the rigid control of the place, so he took off."

Shock straightened my spine. "Is he through the *verða* yet?"

At her nod the tension testing the patience of my wolfy side eased. "Yeah, that's not why I'm worried. We've texted or called each other every day since he left. He wanted me to go with him, but he's a *friend* and I didn't want to give him the wrong impression."

She fell silent. The look of guilt on her face told me to keep quiet and give her the time she needed to go on.

"He got a job up near Libby. He was so excited. But he began calling less and less. On our last video call, I noticed bruises on his neck, bad ones, and a black eye he was trying to hide. When I asked about it, he made a lame excuse to end the call."

Concern ate at me and my resolve to stay quiet.

Candice suddenly stopped picking at the rim of her cup and looked directly at me. "He is a good fighter, so good he could have had a spot in any of the HH packs. Who, or what, can beat up a werewolf with those skills?" she whispered harshly.

The protective part of me wanted to keep her in the dark. But, she was eighteen now, and a very capable young woman who deserved to know everything I did, and more.

"Werewolves, or other shifters." It could be any number of other supe races, but I didn't feel the need to tell her that right now. It would only add to her stress.

"That's what I was afraid of. I need to check on him. I don't want to go alone. Would you come with me?" she asked.

"Of course," I said without hesitation. "That's what friends are for."

The smile she gave me was both wonderful and heavy.

"Thank you so much, Sonya."

Libby was barely two hours north, meaning we could reach it by nightfall. I stood and motioned to my Jeep. "You ready?"

She all but leaped from the bench. "Really? Right now? That's awesome. Yes, of course I am. Thank you so much!"

Letting out a long, relieved breath, she leaned over and hugged me so tight I couldn't breathe. Just as quickly, she pulled away, rose, and grabbed a huge backpack from beside the bench—the kind hikers used when going across the county. I got the impression if I hadn't said yes, she would have gone on her own. I made a vow to myself that as long as I were alive and capable, she would never have to do anything alone.

6

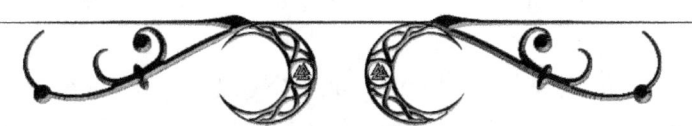

Maybe it was a dirty move waiting to call Ty to let him know where I was going after I was forty minutes into the trip. But, at the time we left he was in the middle of teaching a class and I didn't want to interrupt. That sounded like a good reason, too bad it wasn't the real one. I liked my independence and hated being treated like an orchid. To my surprise, he'd been fairly understanding. Sure, he wanted to come, but when I told him Candice and I needed some girl time and were going to look up a friend of hers, he'd supported the idea. Guilt gnawed at me for giving a partial truth, but I assuaged it by telling myself I'd call him if I even caught a whiff of trouble.

For a solid half hour we listened to the radio, singing along together. Candice surprised me by knowing most of the bluesy music I played. Even more surprising was her amazing singing voice. When the news interrupted and started in on all the wolf attacks in Montana I shut it off. After chatting about everything under the moon besides her issues in Hemlock Hollow I realized Candice wasn't going to say anything if I didn't come out and ask directly. So I did.

"What's up with Hemlock Hollow? You don't seem happy there."

"Aside from all the rules and pack etiquette bullshit?"

I laughed good and hard. "Not that you need more of a reason than that, but I feel like you have another."

One quick, wide-eyed look at me, and then she turned her head toward the passenger window at the snowy landscape passing by. "All the packs want fighters, and I'm not a fighter." She sounded ashamed, and I hated that.

"So what? There is nothing wrong with not being a fighter. I'm not a fighter."

"Yeah, but you're the Frigg blessed seeker." No judgment hid in her tone, just hurt.

"And if I wasn't, they wouldn't want me either, which is why I don't want to belong to any of those packs."

Mouth slightly agape, she turned her head back to look at me. "Really?"

"Really."

She smiled, big and beautiful. "Have I ever told you how awesome you are, Sonya?"

"Yep, but you can tell me as many times as you want."

The remainder of the trip we spent laughing, joking, and engaging in girl talk. Seeing how that wasn't something I got to do very often, it was nice, really nice. Another hour into our trip the snow-cloaked trees to either side of the road gave way to a smattering of small businesses. Candice pulled out her phone and scrolled through her messages. She rattled off the address.

"Take the next left," she instructed.

Easing the Jeep to a crawl so as not to slide on the icy road, I did so. We drove into a neighborhood that began as small houses squatting near one another.

"Do you know anything about this town?" I asked.

One shoulder lifted in a sort of half-shrug. "Not much. It's a human town, for the most part, but from what Fern said about it, there is a decent sized population of werewolves living beneath their noses too."

"Sounds dangerous," I mumbled, mostly to myself.

A snorting noise came from Candice. "Isn't the whole world for us?"

Remembering the media speculating on animal attacks possibly being something more, and pushing me to say I thought so too, I sighed. "Too true."

At Candice's instructions, I took a few more turns and the neighborhood changed from houses to townhouses. Finally, we pulled into the pothole-ridden parking lot of a rundown two-story apartment building that looked like it had been built in the seventies and likely not updated since. I parked beneath the skeletal umbrella of a huge oak tree that had probably been planted the year the complex had been built. Snow covered a roof that sagged in a few spots, and pea green paint bubbled and peeled from the walls. I got out and stood for a moment staring at the place. Nose crinkling against the onslaught of musty odor that wafted all the way across the parking lot, I tried to mouth breathe.

"Are you sure this is it?"

Face pinched, Candice said, "Don't knock it. At least he isn't living on the streets anymore."

"Anymore?"

"Before we both got bitten in we were runaways. That's how we met," she said in a guarded tone that did little to hide her shame.

The tidbit of her past was a tiny treasure, something she didn't offer up easily.

"No knocking here. I just wish I'd known his *verndari* hadn't set him up better to give him a good start in his new life."

Looking up at the apartment building, scanning the numbers on the doors, Candice shook her head. "The guy didn't want him in his pack, and didn't want to help him look at any of the other packs, so Fern didn't want his help."

With Candice leading the way, we started across the parking lot.

"The Hemlock Hollow packs are overrated," I said. Most of the werewolf community disagreed, seeing them as the power houses of the shifter world. "They're too big to be proper packs, proper families. They don't look at new members as people, but as numbers and what they can add to the pack, rather than what the pack can offer them."

Top lip pursing in thought, she looked at me. "I never thought of it that way. That's kind of beautiful," she said.

I shrugged. "I have my moments."

She laughed and punched me playfully in the shoulder. "That you do."

We started up the ice-encrusted metal staircase. It took all of my focus and a solid grip on the railing to stay vertical. The place felt pretty deserted, but then at below thirty degrees, I couldn't really blame people for staying inside as much as possible. Behind several of the apartment doors I heard the soft murmur of heartbeats, muffled conversations, televisions, and clanging of cookware. Candice stopped at the third door from the stairs on the second story. I listened hard, but heard nothing behind it.

Her nostrils flared. "This is the place. But his scent is old," she said.

For a werewolf, my sense of smell left a lot to be desired, so I'd have to take her word for it. Not to mention, these apartments were old, musty, and made me not want to breathe any deeper than necessary. Instead of raising her fist to knock like I thought she would, Candice pulled out two small pieces of metal and set to work on the lock. Before I could protest, the lock clicked and she turned the knob. I gave her a wide-eyed look, but she only shrugged and stepped inside. Not wanting to raise any suspicion, I followed her and quickly shut the door behind me.

I leaned close to her ear just in case we weren't the only werewolves in the building. "This is a bad idea," I whispered.

"He isn't here. Knocking and then breaking in would have been more suspicious," she whispered back.

The studio apartment gave us very little to search. A living room doubling as a bedroom connected to a tiny kitchen where a half-ajar door led to a cramped bathroom. Clothes draped over the frame of the unmade daybed and dishes sat unwashed in the sink. From the smell, he had at least rinsed them and the counters looked wiped down. The place screamed 'bachelor', but not 'slob'. But then, I didn't really know a werewolf who could tolerate the scents of a house messy enough to fall into that category.

"Do you smell that?" Candice whispered.

"You'll have to be a wee bit more specific." Then I did smell it—old, dried, but unmistakable. "Blood," she and I said at the same time.

In a flash of purple and brown hair, she took off for the bathroom. Scanning everything, I followed at a much slower pace. When I poked my head into the bathroom—because there was no way we'd both fit in there—she was picking something out of the tiny garbage can beside the toilet.

It took a hefty amount of control to hold back a chastising, very motherly, comment about why not to touch things in another person's garbage. I didn't bother to suppress my shudder as I softly muttered, "Ew." The wad of toilet paper in her hands was soaked through with crimson.

"It's his blood," she said in a choked voice.

I put a hand on her shoulder and squeezed gently. With a nod, I pointed to the clean counter top, then the spotless tub. "Nothing here indicates that he was in a hurry or desperate, which means he probably isn't running from anyone.

Sucking in a sob, she dropped the toilet paper back in the trashcan. "So he's not running, but maybe he should be. He's hurt and he didn't come to me because I was an idiot and broke his heart."

I turned her toward me. "Hey, no. No guy gets to put the guilt trip on you because you didn't have romantic feelings for him. He is responsible for his own life, and his own choices. You are here now to help as a friend, and that counts for everything," I told her.

Gaze rising to mine, she sniffled. Tears streaked down her cheeks, ruining her eyeliner. "Yeah?

"Hell yeah."

Taking a deep breath, she put her shoulders back, and nodded. "His scent trail is at least a day old here, so what do we do?"

"You don't have any idea where this job of his might be?"

Her shoulders deflated and she shook her head.

"No problem. We'll just look for clues that might lead us to him," I said in a much more optimistic tone than I felt. Detecting wasn't my thing. My failings as a seeker had never felt heavier. But that didn't mean I was about to stop trying.

I took two steps from the bathroom, which put me in the middle of the kitchen. The scent of Chinese take-out led me to the garbage can beneath the left side of the sink. It wasn't terribly overwhelming, mostly because he had emptied and rinsed the containers before tossing them into the trash—clearly not because he was a neat freak, but likely because he was a werewolf and therefore sensitive to strong smells. The little white boxes filled the trashcan, so much so that they were stacked within one another.

"Wow, that's a lot of take-out," I mumbled.

"He loves Chinese food," Candice said.

Loving it was one thing. From the state of his trashcan, this guy lived on it. Then I realized… "These are all from the same restaurant." Of course they were. This tiny town was probably lucky to have *one* Chinese food restaurant.

I turned over one of the folding containers. "Láng's Garden."

Picking up on my train of thought, Candice whipped out her phone and started typing. "It's close to the middle of town, only a few miles away," she said after a second.

Brows rising, I grinned at her. "Feel like trying what falsely passes for Chinese food in a town that probably doesn't have a single authentic Chinese person?"

Halfway through my sentence her mouth opened, but when I finished, she closed it again and gave me a weird look. "Well, I was going to say yes, but after you put it that way…"

I waved it off and started for the door. "No worries. We don't actually have to eat there."

"Good, I think," she said as she followed me.

The moment my boot heals touched the metal balcony in front of the apartment door, an odd bird call, something like a "crawk!" pierced the chilly air. I jumped half out of my skin—claws and fangs extending on instinct. Thankfully, I had the sense to close my mouth in an instinctual attempt to cover my fangs. My hands, I thrust behind my back. Giving me a look, Candice stepped out next to me.

"Jumpy much?"

"Frigg's fertile ovaries, yes. Damn bird scared the hell out of me," I said through a loud exhale.

Scanning the area, I finally found the culprit perched on a bare limb of the oak tree I'd parked the Jeep under. The biggest black bird I've ever seen adjusted its grip on the icy branch. It had to be easily over three feet from its scruffy head to its tail feathers. As it made that weird "crawking" sound again, tufts of feathers expanded out from beneath its chin like a beard. I covered my pounding heart with one hand.

I hoped the thing wasn't a harbinger of some sort of new and horrible doom. It would be just my luck. As a precaution, I gripped the railing tight as I started to descend the stairs. Curtains in one of the apartment windows we passed moved. Feeling eyes on my back, I picked up my pace. By the time Candice and I reached the Jeep, the bird was nowhere to be seen.

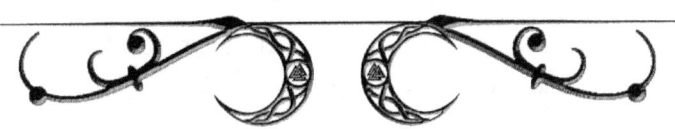

7

Twilight began to descend when we reached Láng's Garden, though the brightness of a snow-covered landscape kept it from being too oppressive. Still, something in the air made me shiver as we got out of the Jeep, and it wasn't the cold. With less than a dozen buildings and only half of those occupied on this secondary road, it didn't exactly feel like 'downtown'. Boards covered the windows of many of the unoccupied buildings. One lonely streetlight half a block away buzzed and flickered as if it had been a bug zapper in a past life and longed for days gone by. From a nearby alley a bird cawed. It startled me, causing me to pull my power in.

The sensation made me realize I should probably do my best to hide it, or the depth of it, at least. Ty's meditations had taught me how to do a rudimentary job of that. Not that his teachings were below par, more like my learning ability was. Still, I could hide my power behind a wall to a degree that normal werewolves couldn't tell I was the seeker if I concentrated hard enough. Alpha level wolves might see right through it. But I'd deal with that problem if it came up.

"Ew. I can't believe this place is his takeout of choice," Candice said as she got out and promptly stepped into an ominous, oily green puddle. I tried to tell myself it was probably that color due to ice melt, but I wasn't buying it. She shook off her red, platform combat boot.

"There is no accounting for taste," I said.

"True. So what now? We just go in and ask around about him?"

Eyes narrowing, lips pursing, I regarded her for a long moment.

"Okay, fine. Bad idea. But what do we do?"

Tugging my blue flannel closed mostly to keep up the appearance of someone affected by the subzero weather, I started across the road to the restaurant. "We go get something to eat. Follow my lead," I said.

Though she groaned and mumbled something critical, she followed.

Surprise rocked me when we stepped inside and the heat I'd been expecting to blast us didn't come. Most businesses kept things a balmy seventy degrees in these parts of Montana during February to entice people to come in out of the cold. It had to be closer to the high fifties in here. Several patrons sitting in the high-backed, overstuffed, red pleather booths still wore their jackets. To our right stood what appeared to double as the cashier and hostess station, the wall behind it painted with an enormous map of China.

Candice reached for the bell sitting on the desk, but I grabbed her hand before she could smack it. "Patience," I said, in no hurry. The longer we had to look around, the more we might see.

A soft, almost imperceptible growl came from her. It made me smile. Not many people had the guts to growl at the seeker. I loved her all the more for it.

"Sorry," she mumbled.

"Don't sweat it. You're worried about your friend. There's nothing to apologize for."

Shoulders dropping as she relaxed, she gave me a short nod. Her attention abruptly veered to the left. Upon following her gaze, I spotted an incredibly well-dressed young man approaching who couldn't be more than a year or two older than Candice. His name tag read Owen. Brownish black hair hung down across his eyes to brush the tops of his cheekbones and give a glimpse of multi-faceted brown eyes. Though those eyes were very telling, it was the press of his power that gave him away as a werewolf, a relatively new one from the feel of it. That didn't shock me so much as the expensive, tailored suit of black on black. To say he was overdressed as a waiter, or even a host, would be a gross understatement. But maybe he was just trying to impress the ladies.

The long, very interested, look he gave Candice made me think I wasn't far off the mark.

"Table for two?" he asked in a smooth, low voice with just the hit of a Boston accent.

Looking at him coyly from beneath her long lashes, Candice gave him a beaming smile that appeared to knock the air right out of him.

"Yep, just two."

They stared into each other's eyes. I suddenly felt like I was interrupting a moment.

With a flourish of his arm, Owen beckoned us to follow him. "Right this way, ladies. I have the perfect table for you."

He led us to the back of the restaurant to a section with nice rice paper dividers printed with traditional Chinese art. Real orchids and white candles sat in the center of the generous table he held a hand toward. Brows rising, Candice slid into the left booth.

"Thanks, Owen."

The man's cheeks flushed slightly. He bowed his head, either in respect, acknowledgment, or just flirting, I wasn't sure.

With far less grace, I plopped down into the right side booth.

From behind his back, Owen produced two menus that looked nothing like the paper ones I'd seen in a slot next to the cash register. Made of cloth and stitched together, these looked downright swanky.

"May I bring some drinks for you while you look over the menus?" he asked.

The very sound of Candice's lips parting made me pop out an answer before she could. "We'll take two ice teas, please. The regular kind, not the Long Island kind."

Face tightening in a properly chastised look, Owen drew back and nodded. "Of course. Coming right up."

As he walked away Candice kicked me beneath the table. "Thanks, mom."

"You're welcome. We need to keep clear heads."

She sighed long and hard, plopped an elbow on the table, and put her chin in her hand. "Yeah, well, a little stress reliever couldn't hurt. And the flirting totally had him convinced not to check my I.D.."

"Yes it could. Using alcohol to relieve stress is a poor coping mechanism that leads to even poorer decisions."

Like any teenager worth their salt, she rolled her eyes at me. "Ugh, that's right, psych degree. Okay, okay, I get it, Doctor Michaelson."

Those last two words cut deep. "I didn't complete my doctorate." I stopped before I could finish with, *and probably never will.*

Snark melting like ice cream in August, she reached across the table and grabbed my hand. "Hey, just because the vampiric system didn't get to drain you completely dry doesn't make you any less brilliant. You're the freaking seeker. That's a pretty amazing way to help people."

A big smile broke across my face. "Act your age and be snarky or something. This insightfulness is downright creepy," I grumbled.

She let go of my hand and leaned back when Owen returned with our drinks. As their eyes snagged, he ducked behind his long bangs, trying to hide a smile that dimpled his reddening cheeks. Gazes still locked, he sat her drink down before her, catching the glass on the edge of her fork and tipping it. With werewolf speed, she reached out and steadied it before it could spill, her fingers coming to rest over his. She giggled and they both let go of the glass at the same time and looked quickly away from one another.

Suddenly I really hoped the tea didn't have sugar in it because I couldn't handle anymore sweetness. They were adorable, but we were here on a mission.

Like a waiter of old instead of today's modern places with digital pads, Owen took out a notepad and pen and looked to me. "What would you ladies like this evening?"

I rattled off my choice, then waited for Candice to tell him hers. After she did, I leaped back in before he could leave. "Hey sir—"

"Oh please." His smile returned with a brilliance that made me acknowledge he was indeed a cute kid. "You ladies can call me Owen."

"Okay, Owen. We're looking up an old student of mine who lives here now, Fernando Ruiz," I began.

Owen stiffened and his face went slack as if he were attempting to hide his emotions.

I went on. "At my insistence, Fern applied for a scholarship before he left. They called me to let me know he got it, but they can't reach him."

The tension eased out of Owen. In my own teen years I'd gotten persuasion down to an art. That coupled with psych classes had taught me how to observe someone and use what I saw to help me know just what to say to get what I needed out of them.

Rolling my hand over, palm up, I finished, "I'd love to give him the good news, but he isn't home, and I don't have his new phone number."

"I've heard the name, of course. Small town." He looked at Candice at the last part. "But I don't know the guy, so sorry, can't help."

Giving a shrug as if she barely cared, Candice batted her lashes at him. "I'll give you my number, in case you hear anything." It didn't seem like an act because it probably wasn't—which made it perfect.

The huge grin he gave her suggested he thought this was the most brilliant idea ever. I had to agree. Now the guy would undoubtably ask around to find a reason to reach out to her.

"Are you ladies going to be in town for a while?" he asked.

"A few days," Candice answered.

"Where you from?" Owen asked. It didn't escape my attention that he had dropped the 'you ladies' part.

"From down south a bit," Candice said, a nice flirting lilt to her voice.

"South like Utah or Wyoming, or…" He let his voice trail off, tone hopeful.

"Nope, just Montana," Candice said.

His werewolf power pulsed, making it clear this news pleased him.

"How about you? Is that a Boston accent?" she asked.

Lips pulling up into an adorable smile, he tried to hide behind his bangs as a blush colored his cheeks. "Yep, first gen. My parents moved there from Ireland just before I was born."

Without any prompting from me, Candice dove into the conversation like a champ. "So what brought you all the way over to Montana?"

Storm clouds stole his smile away. "A series of unfortunate events. But things are looking up," he said, a hint of his smile returning.

Clearly, he wasn't about to give up too much info to a couple of strangers. At least not yet. Not wanting to seem too eager to keep them talking, I cleared my throat.

Eyes widening, Owen straightened and looked quickly over at me. "I'll go get your orders in and put a rush on them," he said.

"No need to rush," Candice said through a sultry smile.

Blushing and grinning fully in return, he dipped his head to us both, turned, and speed walked off.

Brows high, I stared at Candice until she pealed her gaze from Owen's retreating form and finally looked at me.

"What?" she asked.

"Laying it on a bit thick," I whispered.

"Naw. I like him," she admitted.

I leaned over the table and whispered even quieter. "Well he's lying, so be careful."

"How can you tell?" she whispered back.

"He's a werewolf. Fernando is a werewolf. This is a town of mostly humans. There's no way he doesn't know him."

Disappointment furrowed her brow.

"So," I shifted gears. "Tell me about things in Hemlock Hollow. Which heads do I need to shrink to get them to treat you right?"

She laughed. "None. Like you said, their packs are just so big that they're picky about new members. Once

I graduate high school this September I'm going to hit the road."

Anxiety gnawed at me. I hated the idea of her out in this crazy new world on her own as a newbie werewolf. "Well if you want to do me a favor, you are welcome to come to Missoula. I could really use a roommate so I can get a better apartment."

"Why haven't you moved in with that hot professor boyfriend of yours?"

"Because I don't want to rush things and screw them up," I admitted.

A humming noise closer to a purr than a growl rumbled in her chest. "Smart. And hey, maybe a roommate wouldn't be such a bad idea."

Our conversation moved on to more mundane things like how she was doing in school, what classes she liked, how her job at Mike's Malt Shop in Hemlock Hollow was going. She steered away from talk of her life before and I didn't press. I knew enough. Life had been so bad at home that she'd run away two years ago. She had no interest in looking back. Then she'd been attacked by a rogue werewolf and shortly after met me.

While she chatted on with a disturbing amount of passion about her calculus class, I hopped on my phone and booked us a somewhat decent looking motel a few miles away.

Food arrived and after Candice flirted a little more with our waiter, we ate. All the while I listened to the patrons around us. Their conversations were the stuff of everyday life, nothing unusual or remotely supernatural. The only other werewolf in the place who I could feel was Owen. But, this town wasn't like Hemlock Hollow. There weren't thousands of werewolves in it, so I couldn't expect to meet them everywhere I supposed.

Still, something felt off. I couldn't quite put a claw on it.

I paid, Candice and Owen flirted again, then we walked out into the flickering light of a dying streetlamp. Extremely light, small snowflakes fell, the kind that were so thick that in the distance they made it look like fog had settled in.

"Great. Wet fur," Candice said as she pulled her hoodie up over her head.

Laughing, I led the dash across the street to the Jeep. Feathers of creepiness worked their way along my neck and shoulders. I fought down the old instinct to dismiss it. Becoming a werewolf had taught me that to survive we had to unlearn the lessons drilled into us as children to discount and ignore the supernatural. The weird feeling came from the alley between the restaurant and the dark building next to it. Eyes shone from the darkness there—wolf eyes. Driver's door half open, I paused. But before I could decide whether or not to check it out, the eyes, and the energy behind them, disappeared.

8

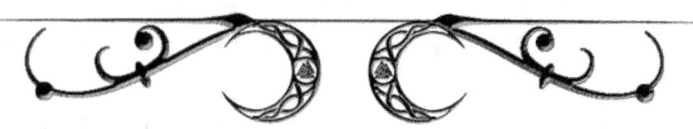

Someone was following us. When headlights kept dogging us after two turns taking a very roundabout way to the hotel, I was sure of it.

"What's up? Your power feels...wonky," Candice said.

"We're being followed."

She glanced in the mirrors, then turned and looked out the back window. "Big black truck from what I can tell. It isn't Fern's style," she said.

"Yeah, I don't think it's him."

Not wanting to lead them to where we were staying, I turned into the parking lot of what looked like a park or a school. A cobbled path gleaming with frost and peppered with granules of snowmelt led around a green space filled with naked deciduous trees. Two very dim, mostly ornamental looking streetlamps scattered around the path cast a golden glow on a mostly snow-covered bench.

"What are you doing? Why are we stopping?" Candice asked, tone panicked.

"It's best to see what they want here rather than lead them back to our hotel."

The sound of her throat working to swallow an impossible lump resounded through the Jeep. "What if what they want is a fight?"

Exuding cool and calm despite feeling the opposite, I smiled as I reached for the door handle. "Then I'll call down lightning and make them realize who they're messing with."

The fear in her power disintegrated and her eyes lit up. She grinned.

"Don't walk all the way up to the truck. Stay out of their reach, just in case. And, on your way up, stop and be obvious about snapping a picture of their license plate with your phone," I told her.

"Gotcha."

We high-fived and hopped out of the Jeep.

The big black truck rumbled to a stop behind us, headlights blinding. Knowing that was their intention, I strode right out of the light up to their driver's door. Candice did as I instructed then stopped near the front bumper. Werewolf power pulsed from the two guys in the cab, enough to put them at *verndari* level or higher.

Fine, that was fine. I could deal with that, I reassured myself, doing my best to keep my own power subdued, hidden.

The driver leaned out the open window, resting an arm on it that bulged in the casing of its gray T-shirt. The sleeve had been rolled up to hold what looked like a pack of cigarettes—which he reeked of. Several days of unshaved brown scruff peppered a tanned face. Brown hair slicked back from a high forehead in a manner that looked greasy from days of going unwashed rather than styled by product. Upper lip curling in disgust at both the smell and fashion faux pas from the seventies, I suppressed a growl.

"You can skip the territorial pissing on my boots act. Before we came here, I checked with the council and they said this is neutral territory," I said, projecting a tiny bit of power into my voice.

Eyes the mixed colors of moss and dirt widened, but he didn't draw back. "And what council might that be, sweetheart?"

The temptation to show a little fang surged, but I resisted. Only alpha level wolves could do that and I didn't want him knowing how powerful I was, yet. "The Hemlock Hollow Alpha Council," I said. It wasn't a lie, exactly. I had asked Ayra, who knew via the council that this was unclaimed territory, and therefore neutral.

His eyes widened enough for me to see white all the way around the irises. Now he did draw back, pulling his arm inside. One thing werewolves everywhere respected was power. And few packs had more numbers, and therefore more power, than those of Hemlock Hollow. Phrasing it to be vague enough to allow him to think I belonged to one of those packs would hopefully be enough. Just showing him my power up front wasn't an option because I'd been told no one had power like mine. Which meant it immediately identified me and that was the last thing I wanted.

The driver looked over at his passenger, another muscular, farm-bred and raised looking young man with a neck as thick as my thigh. A gleam of calculating intelligence shone in this one's eyes, though. Shorn black hair stood straight up in a high flattop that gave him an almost military look. He leaned forward.

"Neutral territory or not, you're gonna find yourselves among a bunch of alpha level wolves here, so you might want to hook up with an escort for your stay," he said.

I put a hand on a hip. "And I guess you're offering to fill that position," I said.

Oily laughter slid from him. "Oh, we're offering to fill much more than that."

"Yeah, we're definitely declining that offer. And my friend here," I hooked a thumb in Candice's direction. She gave them a tight smile and waved. "She just texted that picture she took of your license plate to Sheriff Balderson back in Hemlock Hollow. Just in case you don't understand when a lady declines your offer."

Flattop swallowed hard enough for me to see his Adam's apple work overtime. His glare deepened until he resembled a gunfighter from one of those old western movies. "If Ruiz wanted to be found, you wouldn't have to ask strangers where he is. For your health, I recommend you stop poking around in other people's business," he said through a snarl.

Sucking in a breath, Candice took a step forward. I held a hand up beside my hip, low so these fools would be less likely to see it. She stopped, but the headlights shone on tears in her eyes that pricked my heart.

Gaze narrowing to a knife's edge at me, Flattop growled, leaned back, and smacked Slick in the arm. "Let's get out of here," he grumbled.

"Be seeing yah," Slick said in a menacing tone.

I dropped a bit more of the wall that hid my power. "You better hope not," I warned.

The driver's window whirred up. Slick glared at me through the glass, pointed to his eyes, then to me. Staring him down, I stepped back and dashed away werewolf fast as the engine of the truck revved. I didn't trust the idiot not to run over my feet. They tore out of the parking lot in reverse, ran over the curb, and slid sideways on the icy road, nearly hitting the only light post on the street before tearing off, rear end fishtailing.

Dancing with the danger of slipping in the icy parking lot, I speed walked to the Jeep and jumped in. Candice was already buckling up before I turned the engine over. I didn't want to say it out loud and scare her, but I wanted out of there before they could circle around and follow us again.

I was certain of two things. Something was up with the werewolf population in this town. And that wouldn't be the last we saw of Slick and Flattop.

Candice didn't say a word until we checked into our hotel room with two queen beds squeezed into the same little room.

"They knew his name," she whispered as she paced the three foot isle before the beds that led to the bathroom.

I threw my blue duffle bag on the bed closest to the window. Though we were up on the second story, that didn't mean much. Werewolves could jump like nobody's business. I wanted Candice as far away from any potential danger as I could get her, meaning I took the drafty bed with a view of snow-topped pine trees.

"They did," I said.

"Do you think they are the ones who hurt him?" she asked in a small voice. "Do you think they did again? He could be laying injured somewhere, or..."

Fast enough to risk breaking an ankle, I flew across the room and took her by the shoulders. Tears glistened so thick in her eyes I knew she wasn't seeing me as we locked gazes. "No. Don't go there. We are not going there."

Lips pulling up into an 'o' shape, she blew out a long breath and slowly nodded. I nodded with her and rubbed up and down her arms. "Go, freshen up. I'm going to call Ty. Afterwards, we can go for a walk and get some air and sniff around. How's that sound?"

"Good," she said on another long exhale.

I kept my smile glued in place until she crossed the room and closed the bathroom door behind her. Shaking my head, I drew a hand through my long, black hair. Things had almost gone really sideways and no one knew we were here. Ty and Ayra had an idea, but I hadn't told them any details. While I valued my independence, I had to admit to myself if no one else, that keeping Ty in the dark about this trip had been both a bad idea, and unfair to him.

Swallowing my pride, I pulled my phone out of my pocket and called him. After five rings it went to voicemail. I kept my voice upbeat and positive as I told him exactly where we'd gone, a less alarming version of why, where we were staying, and that we planned to be back in another two days. It being the middle of the week, I felt pretty confident he wouldn't white knight up here since he had classes to teach. As an extra precaution, I let him know I'd call him in the morning when I got up. A timeframe of check in calls would both keep him from worrying, and keep Candice and I safer—just in case.

The sink in the bathroom turned off and Candice came out. "That was smart, calculated. He'll leave us alone unless we don't check in, but will come for us if something happens. And you said you weren't good at math." Of course she'd heard me on the phone. Werewolf hearing and all that. I should have known.

Laughing, I threw an arm around her shoulders and turned her toward the door. "Let's go, math whiz."

"I'm glad you didn't say 'math geek', it's derogatory," she teased as we walked out into the overheated hallway.

"I would never say anything derogatory to someone smarter than me."

A razzberry vibrated from her lips. "Says the psych major. And you'd never say anything derogatory about anyone."

We exited a side door and carefully descended an icy looking set of stairs along the side of the building. The snow had all but stopped, becoming those super fine crystals the light had to hit for one to see. It was so pretty it made me smile, and wish Ty were here to share the sight with. The thought made me uneasy. I wasn't used to wanting to share moments with a guy. I liked it, but that only made the unease grow.

Candice shook me from my musings. "But thanks for the vote of confidence. So what are we sniffing around for?" she asked, breath puffing white in the cold night.

An only slightly less icy sidewalk greeted us. For appearances sake, I buttoned my flannel closed and stuffed my hands in the pockets of my jeans. No sense in drawing any more attention than we already had.

"Maybe Fernando's trail, I hope. It's a small town. Those creeps don't want us finding him for some reason, which makes me think he's out here somewhere," I said.

"And you think we're close?"

"Yep."

Candice developed a spring in her step that had me worrying for her footing on the treacherous sidewalk. "Gods, if I were only half as smart as you are! You're amazing."

I smacked her arm so she'd look at me and get the full effect of my glare. "Don't say that. You are extremely smart, smarter than me in a lot of ways. What kind of crap are they filling your head with in Hemlock Hollow High?"

Laughing, and almost making it sound convincing, she smacked me back. "Naw, that's old childhood trauma baring it's fangs."

"Good, because I was going to have to kick some tails if that was the case. You are smart, capable, and amazing, and don't let anyone tell you any different," I pressed.

The smile that lit up her face banished some of the shadows beneath her eyes. Moments later she hid the smile behind a stern look. "Whatever." But her flippant tone and roll of her eyes couldn't hide the joy that radiated from her power.

Our wanderings had taken us a few blocks down and over, out of the neighborhoods and into an industrial part of town. Steel and brick buildings rose on either side of the road. The sidewalk beneath our feet had deteriorated to crumbled concrete in some places, gravel in others. It actually made for better traction considering the ice and snow. Why we ended up here, I wasn't sure. My feet had just wanted to come this direction, so I'd allowed them to lead me.

The cry of an angry bird cut through the night sharp as a knife. No, not just angry—in pain. Before I could even think about it, my feet sped in the direction of the sound. Less than half a block away I came to the beginning of an alley tucked between tall buildings. A guy crouched, peering beneath a big metal dumpster, and another stood slapping a baseball bat into his hand. They smelled and felt familiar—Flattop and Slick.

"Come on, pull it out from under there and toss it my way!" Flattop said over the thwack of the bat against his hand.

With a grunt, Slick shoved the dumpster—which had to weigh close to four thousand pounds—aside. Sometimes the strength of our kind still blew my mind. A huge black bird cowered against the building as if trying to disappear into the brick. One wing hung at an odd angle down by its side. Seeing it sent a wave of rage burning through me. Slick reached for the poor creature.

"What on Muspelheimr do you think you're doing?" I roared as I strode into the alley.

Lucky for him, his hand stilled.

"Oh shit," Candice muttered behind me.

Top lip curled away from his fangs, Slick rose and turned toward me. The bird hopped a few feet away from him, damaged wing dragging the ground. The sight hit the embers of my rage like a shot of Bacardi 151. Huge, fluffy flakes of snow began to fall. *Damnit.* I knew the signs all too well—a storm was being drawn to my heightening power. I had not wanted to reveal my cards like this.

"Well, well. Someone was hiding their true power," Flattop said as he turned to me. His muddy eyes looked me up and down as though he wanted to devour me.

In contrast, Slick's gaze darted about as if looking for an exit. I wouldn't have pegged him for the smarter one. Who knew?

The bird went very still, looked straight at me, and let out a querulous sounding "Crawk?" I swore I could hear the pain in its voice. No, not it, him. Something deep inside told me that with profound certainty.

"Come get a taste of it, Flattop," I said to keep their attention away from the bird.

Chuckling to himself as if this nickname pleased the hell out of him, Flattop started my way, once again slapping the bat into his hand.

"I don't like this. She has the power of an alpha," Slick called as he took a step backward. The alley ended in a brick wall that had to be eight feet tall. As a werewolf he'd be able to jump it, but who knew what lay on the other side. Regardless, he looked like he wanted to try.

Flattop rolled his shoulders. "So what? So do I," he said, flashing a smile that showed teeth speckled with chew.

"Gross," Candice mumbled behind me.

I hated to break it to Flattop, but his power wasn't up to the level of the alphas I knew.

"Someone who would harm a defenseless creature has no business being an alpha," I said.

He made a rude noise with his lips. "The strong rule the weak," he said.

"Ruling doesn't involve harming those less powerful than yourself," I said.

Another rude noise came from him. "Clearly you don't know your history, or the nature of our kind."

One more step took me within four feet of him and his dimpled bat. "Clearly you don't know the culture of my people, or you wouldn't dare hurt a raven." I was taking a wild stab at it being a raven. For all I knew, it could have been a crow. But I thought I remembered something about ravens being bigger, and this fellah was as big a bird as I'd ever seen—bigger even than an eagle. I didn't think ravens were supposed to get that big, but what did I know?

Eyes narrowing, Flattop peered Slick's way, shook his head, then looked back at me. "What, Indians?"

Fangs extended, forcing my jaws apart. I'd dealt with too many jerks like him as a kid. "No, moron. Indians are from India. The term you're looking for is Native American. But no, you're still wrong. I'm talking about my Swedish side."

An abrupt, horrible guffaw shot from him. "You're half Swede, really? I never would have guessed that."

As if I needed any more motivation to pummel him. "Walk away, now," I advised him, pouring a little power into the words.

Hands held up like the thug he was, Slick nodded emphatically and began to slip past me toward the main street. I didn't like him getting closer to Candice, but the fear on his face told me he wasn't trying to flank us.

"Where do you think you're going?" Flattop snapped.

"Away?" Slick made the word a question, as if he wasn't sure why he was walking. But he didn't stop.

"Coward! Get your ass back here. It's just a couple of women," Flattop said.

Slick shook his head, eyes going so wide they became predominately white. "That one isn't. She's more than she looks like. I ain't messing with the likes of her."

"Whatever. Leave if you're chicken shit." Flattop twirled the bat around. "I could use the practice before tomorrow's match."

Rapid footfalls slapped on the hardpacked snow behind us as Slick abandoned his companion at a rapid rate. Just to be sure, I glanced over my shoulder. Standing at the opening of the alley, Candice did the same, then looked back at me and nodded. Good. We were down to one. I could take one. At least, I hoped I could. And, as much as I wanted to razz him about needing the bat, it would give me an advantage against him.

Without any kind of warning, he lunged forward and swung at me with all his might. Great, a jerk and a dirty fighter. Even as I thought this, I ducked and drove a sidekick straight for his kidney. I connected, hard, while the bat only hit the wall of the building—just like

I had planned. The impact and kick combined to stun him long enough for me to chamber my leg and whip it back out in a hook kick that struck the back of his head. He went down fast and hard. Normally I'd never use a hook kick to someone's head because it could be lethal. But werewolves weren't like humans. And he had really pissed me off.

Instead of getting up and coming for me again, the bastard scampered across the snow packed ground toward the raven.

"No!" I screamed, pushing power into it and making it a command.

He froze, hand out, fingers inches from the cowering bird's broken wing. Not waiting to see how long my influence over him lasted, I jumped and landed between him and the bird. Claws extended, I slashed at his arm. As he drew away, my claws gouged four deep gashes across his forearm. Steaming blood dripped into the snow.

"Touch him again and I will cut your arm off," I warned through a furious growl. To my own surprise, I meant it. While I didn't like violence, I was willing to dole it out to those who hurt animals or kids.

The raven looked around my leg and squawked at the guy as if he understood and was emboldened by my words. Growling, Flattop bounded to his feet and squared off with me again.

Snow fell so hard around us at this point that had he been more than ten feet from me, I wouldn't have been able to see his expression.

"You shouldn'ta cut me, bitch," he said.

I'd never liked being called a bitch. Ever since becoming a werewolf, it straight up infuriated me. Brandishing my claws, I let out a growl filled with all the rage this idiot was stirring up. Eyes shooting open wide, his head pulled back. Again I growled, this time pulling at the power of the storm building in the sky above me. Lightning crackled somewhere in the snow overhead, making the night blindingly bright for a moment.

"What *are* you?" Flattop asked, taking a big step backward.

"More than you can handle."

Lightning brightened the sky again, not quite reaching through to me yet, but it was close, so close. One more pull on the storm's power and it might come.

Throat working hard, Flattop dropped the bat. As it clattered on the ice, he turned and ran. He slipped, fell hard, scrambled up, and kept running—right past a figure standing at the entrance to the alley. Eyes huge, mouth dropped open wide, Owen the waiter stared at us, not even glancing Flattop's way as he passed.

Finally, he found his voice. "Wow. That was amazing."

I let out a long sigh and the snowfall decreased to a flake or two here and there.

"You haven't seen nothing yet," Candice said through a laugh.

A bird's croak of pain drew my attention away from them. The black bird looked up at me with what felt like a curious expression. Deep pain darkened its odd honey and cinnamon eyes—eyes with no sclera, though that part seemed normal enough for birds from what I'd read. The bright irises, I wasn't so sure about. Crouching down to his level, I reached out slowly, offering my hand. For what, I had no idea. It would serve me right if he bit me. And if he did, that was fine. If it gave him a feeling of power after being victimized, I would gladly make the sacrifice of a bit of flesh. For a moment I thought he might as he tried to sink into the brick wall. A small sound of pain came from him that pierced my heart.

I drew my hand back. "No, no. You don't need to pull away. Don't hurt yourself more for me," I pleaded.

His head cocked to the side, a beard of feathers fanning out beneath his chin. This close, I realized he stood as tall as mid-thigh level to me. I took a step back before kneeling on the ice a few feet away. "That's a good, big boy. You get to call the shots, bud, not me."

Eyes blinking slowly, clearly taking me in, his head cocked the other direction. He leaned away from the wall, then took a stumbling step in my direction, limping on one leg, left wing dragging on the ground beside him. The sight brought tears to my eyes and made me want to chase down Flattop and break a few of his bones. Hands on my knees, I waited, letting the bird come to me. And he did, one painful, slow step at a time. Soon, his beak reached out and nudged my right hand.

"There's a boy. See, it's okay. I won't hurt you. And I won't let anyone else either," I said softly.

An interesting noise somewhere between a coo and a croak vibrated from him, making his throat feathers flare. Slowly, I lifted my hand and stroked his chest. He ducked his head under my fingers and rubbed against my palm. Silky soft feathers tickled me, but I didn't pull away. Without me calling it, my power flared up and flowed over the bird. Eyes widening, he looked up at me and froze. The flow continued. A power all his own reached out of him and met mine. The two mingled in a way I'd only ever seen and felt my power do with Ty's and Ayra's. It felt odd, but not bad, kind of like weaving an intricate sailor's knot. Why that image came to mind, I had no idea.

To my complete surprise, the bird's wing hanging on the ground moved, righted itself, then tucked in against his side. Eyes widening as if this surprised him just as much, his head popped up, he took a step back, and flapped his wings carefully as if testing them out. The strong flapping blew my hair back. Unreadable as his face was all covered in feathers, somehow I could still detect the joy in his expression. Those wings had to span at least five feet. Still flapping, he hopped forward, making happy crawking sounds followed by odd popping noises made with his beak.

On a wave of relief, laughter flowed from me. "Quite the vocabulary you've got there fellah," I said.

As if in answer, he launched into a series of crawks and chitters that almost sounded human in origin as he alighted upon the dumpster. Claws scratched for purchase as he slid along the snow-covered lid, wings out in an attempt to find balance. I lunged forward to catch him, thinking he might still be hurt, but he caught himself on the rounded lip of the lid just before sliding off. Feathers ruffling, he settled atop the lid and looked at me with an expression I would have sworn was sheepish.

Last summer, with Ayra's help, I'd been able to heal using a blend of our unique power. But it had required channeling lightning. How I'd managed to heal this bird without it, I had no idea.

"Whoa. I thought his wing was broke," Candice said, moving up behind me.

I shrugged as I stood. "Maybe it wasn't."

Owen, who had also moved closer during my encounter with the bird, gestured toward me. "It definitely was, like compound fracture broken. I can still smell the blood. You healed it using something that felt like packbond power," he said.

Brow furrowing, Candice looked from him to me. "That shouldn't be possible, right? It's a bird."

"Definitely not. I've never heard of anything like it," Owen said.

I sighed. "Yeah, well, that's on par for me. What are you doing here Owen?"

He blushed and tried to duck his chin into the raised collar of his brown leather jacket. "Oh, yeah, well, um…" Looking everywhere but at either myself or Candice, he ran a hand through his brown, snow speckled hair." Finally, his gaze settled on Candice. "My boss heard me talking to you and took the piece of paper with your number on it. So I came to give you mine," he said, brightening.

Though he seemed genuine enough, my suspicious nature didn't allow me to be convinced. "And you just randomly came across us in the industrial part of town," I said, letting my disbelief leak through my words.

Confirming my suspicions, he looked away. "Well, not exactly…"

"I'm not in the mood Owen. You'd better be straight with me," I warned.

The bird behind me squawked as if to emphasize my warning.

Owen's eyes grew wider. "Fascinating."

Candice laughed, whether at him or the bird, I wasn't sure.

A slight growl from me snapped him back to attention.

"I saw those guys tail you when you left the restaurant." Again, his gaze shifted to Candice. "They're bad news. I wanted to make sure you were okay."

My suspicion started to melt as I realized his interest in her was genuine. Still, he rankled me, probably because I was still itching for a fight. "Thanks, but we little women can handle ourselves," I grumbled.

Hands up, he shook his head. "I have no doubt about that. I didn't come to play shining knight. I'm a cook, not a fighter." Again he looked at Candice. "Though I would have tried if needed. I bet you can probably fight better than I can," he said through a nervous laugh. "And I definitely would have called what passes for werewolf authorities here if needed."

Candice blew air between her lips. "I'm no fighter either. Sonya here doesn't like violence, but she can do some seriously—"

"Okay, that's enough sharing," I interrupted. "You're a waiter and a cook?" I asked Owen.

Lips pinching into a look of annoyance, he ducked his head, making his hair fall across his face and hide his expression. "Just a waiter. My specialty is barbeque. Boss didn't want anything like that in his restaurant."

Grinning, Candice walked up to him and tagged him playfully in the arm. "I love barbeque! Your boss doesn't know what he's missing."

"Right?" Owen asked.

They laughed and started from the alley together. It did my heart good to see her happy, especially considering how stressed she'd been earlier. Unsure of what the rest of this trip would hold for us, I let her have her moment. Half expecting him to be gone, I looked back at the bird. Still atop the trashbin, he watched me with his head cocked.

"I don't really understand how, but I'm glad you're okay," I said.

Wings flapping, he let out an emphatic, "Crawk-crawk!"

Concerned Flattop might have pent up rage he wanted to vent and come back, I felt reluctant to leave the bird behind. "Well, since your wing is healed, you should leave now. Go somewhere safe," I told him as if he could understand me. Maybe he could. I remembered hearing somewhere that crows and ravens were smart.

With two powerful flaps of his wings, he took to the air, rose up, and disappeared into the snowy night. Something heavy settled over my heart at his departure. Maybe it was just residual stress from this bizarre day. Shaking it off, I turned and walked from the alley. When I reached the street, Candice stood waiting beneath the block's only streetlight and Owen was walking backwards half a block away waving at her.

I shook my head. "That fool is going to fall on his ass."

Slipping on the ice, he nearly did just that. He turned red as Fireball when he saw me, then spun on his heel, shoved his hands in the pockets of his leather bomber jacket, and marched away.

Candice let out a good-natured chuckle. "Don't tease him. I think he's adorable. He was keeping an eye on me until you got here," she said.

Charmed by the sheer joy on her face, I smiled as I turned and started back the way we'd come. "I have to admit, he is pretty adorable." What I didn't say was that my gut and psychology classes told me he was hiding something. "You got his number, right?"

Red that had nothing to do with the cold tinged her cheeks. "I did."

Good. Because I had a feeling, before this was over, we'd be talking to Owen again.

9

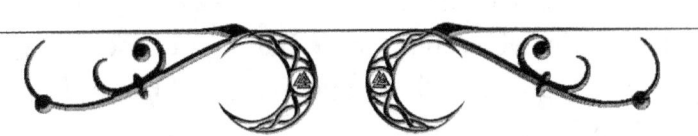

We took our time walking back, hoping to catch Fernando's scent. Well, Candice hoped to catch his scent. I had zero hopes of smelling anything distinguishable beneath the one-inch blanket of new snow that had fallen. But I kept my ears peeled, partially because it was my best sense, and partially because sound traveled better in cold temperatures. Time and again I heard a soft 'whooshing', most likely the wind blowing through the leafless trees. But when a weird chittering followed by a "clop, clop, clop," echoed through the cold, dark streets, I stopped in my tracks.

"What the…?" I mumbled as I turned and looked slowly around.

On the top of a used bookstore sign a few buildings behind us sat a dark shape nearly three feet in height. I squinted, trying to make out the silhouette within the darkness. Without any backlight, it was nearly impossible. But only nearly. I focused my power into my sight. The silhouette took shape; a long, thick beak, a scruff of feathers beneath, and a bell-shaped tail.

"Huh," Candice said. "Looks like I'm not the only one who made a friend tonight."

Something deep inside told me without a doubt this was the bird I'd saved. The sight of him brought a sense of calm and relief. It wasn't that I'd been worried about him, more like part of me had been afraid I wouldn't see him again and had been deeply bothered by that.

"Hey fellah," I said.

He made a bird noise that sounded suspiciously like he was trying to copy the inflection of my voice. It made me smile. Knowing most animals took teeth baring as aggression or a desire to have them for dinner, I made sure to keep my lips closed. Wings spread, he glided to the next closest store sign. The horrible scrape of talons on metal screeched through the night as he scrambled to get a grip, failed, and nearly fell from the sign. On instinct, I darted forward and held my hands out to catch him. At the last moment, he found his grip and clung on.

"Oh no, are you still hurt?" I asked.

A series of popping and gurgling noises came from him that only served to worry me more.

"If he answers you in English, I'm outa here," Candice said.

Fluffing up, he righted himself and managed to look quite indignant.

Candice let out a sharp laugh. "I think he's just clumsy."

"Or the poor thing is still rattled from being hit by a bat," I said.

At the sound of my voice his head cocked one way, then the other.

A very loud, very long yawn sounded from Candice. I felt for her. It had to be past midnight. Weariness wore me down as well, though I had become adept at ignoring it. Nodding to the bird, I started in the direction of our hotel again.

The loud and insistent, "Crawk!" the bird made stopped me in my tracks.

I looked up at him. He had puffed up, all his feathers rising until he looked twice his size—which was saying a lot. Another "Crawk!" issued from him before he turned and leaped from the sign. He soared across the street and landed on the top of the stop sign.

"Huh. I think he wants us to follow him," Candice said.

We exchanged dubious looks. The bird called out to us again. Deep inside, the urge to follow him nagged at me.

"Why not? What do we have to lose?" I asked as I started in his direction.

"Sleep," Candice murmured.

Reluctant as she seemed, her soft footsteps sounded behind me. "This is crazy," she grumbled as she walked.

Ahead our feathered friend soared from store sign to store sign, barely alighting long enough on each to even call it landing. I had a feeling that had more to do with his lack of balance than any desire to hurry. Every now and then he glanced back to make sure we still followed.

"Probably," I agreed. "But we have nothing to lose at this point."

"There's plenty to lose, like the feeling in my feet," she said as she caught up to me.

"You're a werewolf. The cold won't bother your feet."

She stuck a platform booted foot out and rotated her ankle. "Have you seen these things? I don't mean from the cold."

I waved a hand. "Yeah, but who needs feeling in your feet when you look that fabulous?"

Nodding, she kept pace with me. "True."

In the time it took to walk another two blocks, the snow stopped. The chill in the air cut through my blue flannel, meaning it had to have dropped below zero. Above that and I didn't notice it much. That, along with a need for better traction than my boots could provide, made me long to shift into wolf form. But, considering this town was made up of mostly humans, no way could we take that risk. Being able to shift in town was the one thing Hemlock Hollow had going for it. Okay, maybe not the only thing, since two of my best friends lived there.

Our bird guide led us out of the industrial part of town and past several open fields. When we reached a skeletal looking tree he'd chosen as his latest perch and he flew down a dirt road with knee deep ruts packed with ice and snow, Candice grabbed my arm and stopped me from following.

"Okay, it's been a nice trip to crazy town, but I think we should go back to our hotel now," she said. An edge of fear added a sharpness to her voice that made me realize just how far out we'd come.

To one side of the road stretched a field of white, on the other side rose evergreens mixed with barren deciduous trees. The side road the bird had flown down meandered into the trees, bending to the right to disappear into them. After the icy welcome we'd already received from some of the locals, it suddenly seemed like a very bad idea to explore any further off the beaten path. In fact, going anywhere but straight back to the hotel had been foolish.

What had compelled me to follow a bird into the cold, dark, unknown, Frigg only knew. But even now I felt a powerful pull deep inside. It urged me to follow him. It actually took quite some effort to keep my feet from moving in his direction.

"You're right. Let's head back," I said, forcing myself to turn away.

We only got two steps before Candice came to such an abrupt halt that she slid a few inches on the icy road.

Nose in the air, her head turned in the direction of the dirt road.

"What is it?" I whispered.

"Fern. I smell him."

Dark brows furrowing so deep I could see them out of the top of my vision, I gave her a long look. "Don't tell me, down the road the bird flew."

"Okay I won't tell you," she said as she started walking toward that very road.

I should have been used to the weirdness scale tipping deeper into the freaky, but what could I say? Life still surprised me.

Blowing out a breath, I grabbed her hand and pulled her along the edge of the road, near the treeline. "Let's try to stay out of plain sight."

She nodded in agreement. Thankfully, the snow was low and packed enough that it was fairly easy traveling. The soft crunchy layer on top actually helped with traction. Two trees ahead of us, on our side of the road, the big black bird perched amidst the pine boughs, staring back at us.

"Yeah, we get it. We're coming," I whispered.

He made soft bird noises in response. As we grew closer he hopped to the next tree, and then the next, just like the signs back in town. I began to feel like I was following a rabbit down a hole that just kept getting deeper.

The twisty road wound through tall fir trees and spindly aspen, all of which grew so close together and rose so high into the night sky that they effectively blocked us from seeing what lay ahead. Foreboding scraped up my spine. We were following a bird, after all.

"Do you still smell him?"

Candice nodded. "It's getting stronger."

Shaking my head, mostly at myself, I looked up at the bird. "Alrighty then, lead on."

Head dipping my direction, his black feathers flapped against the cold air as he did as I bid. Just as we reached a bend in the road, I felt the tickle of the power of other werewolves—a lot of them. I heard the roar and crackle of a bonfire maybe a hundred yards or so away. Shouts of encouragement, challenge, derision, growls, and whoops and hollers carried to me on the air. From the sounds, I'd guess anywhere from sixty to a hundred or so people gathered. Beneath the cheers and jeers, I heard grunts of exertion and the slap of flesh on flesh—a fight.

Nose going up, Candice's steps paused. "I smell…sweaty men."

A deep reluctance to continue any further made me ask, "Do you still smell Fernando?"

"Definitely, and it's a fresh scent trail. He's here."

Perched directly above us, the black bird croaked softly, urgently. I looked up to see him looking down at me. So much for turning back. Up ahead, maybe ten feet off the road, rose an eight-foot-tall cyclone fence topped with coils of razorwire.

"What the hell?" I whispered.

Somewhere beyond that fence I felt the pull of a newly bitten losing their battle with madness. On instinct, my gaze drifted skyward. A scattering of clouds mostly hid the half full moon suspended in the midnight blue sky. I had time. Knowing that failed to quell the urgency that always rose whenever I felt the chaotic power of a werewolf who needed my help. I wanted to charge that fence and leap over it. The urge was so strong my legs quivered.

"I don't like this," Candice said, gaze on the fence.

The thing wouldn't keep werewolves in or out. I could easily jump ten feet high with just a few steps of a running start, and I was one of the least physically gifted werewolves I knew. No. This fence was meant to keep curious *humans* out.

"Me neither, but we can't turn back."

Candice's chest rose and fell with a deep breath, she shoved her hands in her pockets, and nodded. We kept walking with the bird leading the way.

"You said Fernando already shifted, and that he has control of his wolf, right?" I asked.

"Yeah. Why?"

"Because there is someone here who hasn't."

"You mean a condemned?"

"No," I answered too quickly, too harshly. I hated thinking of them that way before they'd had a chance to make peace with their wolf. It felt too much like giving up on them. "Just a troubled newly bitten who hasn't turned yet."

"It's so cool that you can feel the difference between someone who hasn't turned yet and someone who has," Candice mused, voice filled with awe.

The conversation distracted me so much that we rounded a bend and came upon a gate without me even feeling the two werewolves in human form who leaned against the concrete pillars to either side of it, chatting. Thankfully, I'd been suppressing the feel of my power since turning down the road.

Our bird guide pulled up short in his flight and nearly smacked right into a tree limb before recovering and landing in a graceless heap.

The two men straightened and turned to us, bodies tense with deadly readiness. Both wore jeans, pull-on style cowboy boots, and light jackets over their broad frames. The one on the right sported a long brown ponytail, possessed a strong, Romanesque nose, clean shaven square jaw, and his eyes were narrowed to slits beneath bushy brows that nearly connected. His slightly shorter companion smiled at us. Shaggy, dark hair half hid his eyes which glowed ever so slightly in the dark. Both exuded the power of mid-level pack members.

"Hey ladies. You're a bit late to watch the fights. Last one is in process now. You come for the after party?" Shaggy asked. His tone, combined with the slow way his gaze traveled over me, made it clear what he was hoping our answer would be.

"We did," I said in my flirtiest voice—which came out too high-pitched and giggly.

Ponytail pushed away from the stone pillar and crossed his arms over his chest. "Well I don't recognize you." He pulled a cellphone from his back pocket and brought something up on it, the light making his face glow. "Are you on the list?"

I didn't dare give him our real names. Just because I helped those in need didn't mean other werewolves liked having me around—and most of them knew my name, if nothing else about me. Some saw what I did as meddling in their pack business, undermining their authority. And, confrontation was something I liked to avoid when possible.

"I didn't know there was a list. I thought anyone could come party," I said, pushing my bottom lip out in what I hoped was a cute pout.

Shaggy let out a long, disappointed sigh. "Sorry, doll. I'm afraid it's invite only."

Inwardly I bristled. No one but Ty got to call me pet names. But my irritation made it easier to look disappointed. Before I could try to charm my way in, footsteps crunched on the frozen ground on the other side of the gate, approaching. A familiar figure stepped out of the darkness of the forest beyond.

"Owen," Candice called with no small measure of relief in her voice.

Ponytail turned to stare at Owen from beneath raised brows.

"Hey ladies. They're with me, guys," he said. I had to give the guy props for thinking on his feet.

"You know the rules, Mic. They aren't on the list, they don't get in," Ponytail said through a sneer that made him look like he had no upper lip. His derisive, talking down tone made me want to stomp on his foot.

The ever-so-slight tightening of his smile was the only indication the man's attitude bothered Owen. "You gonna open the gate so I don't have to jump over and risk slipping on the ice when I land?"

"Nope. I want to see that," Ponytail said in all seriousness.

Shaggy smacked him in the arm, hard. "Don't be an ass." He turned and pressed a series of buttons on a panel on the concrete pillar. The gate clunked and then slid open.

Giving Shaggy a genuine smile, Owen walked through. "Thanks, man."

"No problem. Don't mind him." Shaggy thrust a thumb in Ponytail's direction. "His mamma shifted when she was pregnant with him."

Red faced, Ponytail growled. "Stop telling people that. You know it ain't true."

Laughter tumbled from Owen as he and Shaggy bumped fists. The amount of testosterone in the air began to give me a headache. Gaze sparkling, partially from the predator in the night thing and partially with something else, Owen put an arm around both Candice and I and turned us away from the gate. He started walking and I didn't resist, sensing we were on treacherous ground here. I snaked an arm around his back. Clearly he had information we needed and I wasn't about to let him get away without telling us.

The sound of air moving against feathers reached me. I looked up to see the black bird soaring above us, following. He squawked and made odd popping noises that I would have sworn were protests.

"Damn, what the hell, Mic?" Ponytail called from behind us.

Knowing many Irish people, and people of Irish descent, hated that slur, I tensed, fangs clenched against a retort. I wanted to punch him in the mouth for it. But the way Owen studiously ignored him made me realize I might make matters worse if I gave into the instinct. Instead I settled for casting a dark glare over my shoulder.

"The man has more game than you give him credit for," Shaggy said.

They teased and heckled one another, their voices growing quieter as we walked away. Owen and Candice exchanged pleasantries about how good the other looked, a natural enough sounding conversation. I waited until the guards' voices faded away completely and we were a good ways back down the road.

I stepped out from under Owen's arm and continued walking down the side of the road. Giving him fierce stink eye, I crossed my arms over my chest and marched on. It was too soon to ask all the questions I wanted to ask. Sound carried far too well on cold air, and werewolves hearing was far too good. Candice stayed tucked under his arm, which was fine by me, good, even, considering she had an arm around his waist and could stop him from dashing away if needed. But the flushed, content look on his face told me that wouldn't be a problem.

Once we reached the main road and I couldn't hear any other werewolves, I turned to Owen. "Out with it. What is that place?"

The bird soared down so low I thought for a minute he might try to land on my shoulder.

Eyes widening, Owen glanced around. "Whoa. That bird is totally following you now."

Candice slid away from him. Lips pursed, she pressed, "Spill."

He held his hands up in surrender as he kept walking. "In my defense, at first I thought you ladies knew about the ranch."

"Why would you think that?" I asked.

"You came to the restaurant."

"So?" Candice made it a question.

"So, that's where our kind go to get into the ranch," he said.

"If that's true, why didn't you say something about it then?" I asked.

Head cocking to the side, he pursed his lips. "Because you didn't ask. The rule is, if they don't ask, they don't know, and if they don't know, don't tell them."

"I'm asking now. What's the ranch?" I said through gritted teeth.

The bird circling overhead squawked as if to emphasize my urgency. Owen stared at him out of the corner of his eye. "That's fair. The ranch is where lone wolves go to blow off some steam without the consequences of pack standing."

"You mean they go there to fight," I said.

"Oh my Freya. Fern could be there," Candice said. She dashed in front of him, stopping him in his tracks, and grabbed him by the jacket. "Is he there?"

Hands held up, he gaped for words for several seconds before getting them out. "I truly don't know. I wasn't lying. I only go to deliver food, not to see the fights. It isn't my thing."

"Are these fighters there of their own free will?" I asked.

"Yeah, absolutely."

The expression on his face showed no signs of deceit, and neither did his power. But, just because he believed a thing was true didn't make it true, especially if he didn't watch the fights.

"I need you to get me in there," I said.

"Us," Candice pressed.

Face scrunching into an apologetic look, he shrugged. "I don't have that kind of power. Like I said, I just bring the food in."

"Then we'll help you bring the food in."

"It doesn't work that way. Theo hires everyone and he'd never let a random 'helper' in, sorry," Owen said, grimacing like it hurt him to say the words.

The desperation in Candice's eyes when she grabbed my arm pinched at my heart. "We have to get in. I know Fern's in there, I just know it," she whispered.

Taking her hand in mine, I turned to Owen. "How do we get invited?"

"Two ways, as a fighter, or they are always looking for more ladies in the crowd."

"We'll take the latter," I said quickly.

Lips pressed together, Owen tapped them as he thought. "I can for sure get you in next Friday."

Today being Friday, a week out didn't work for me, not when there was a newly bitten in there who needed my help, and Fern, of course. "No. Get me in there tomorrow."

"Us," Candice grumbled.

Owen grimaced. "Tomorrow is mid and heavy weight fighters, and exceptional matches at the end. It's a really popular night. Boss only let's a small amount of spectators in and spots fill up fast. Gotta keep things quiet so we don't attract the attention of the neighbors. I might not be able to get you in that way tomorrow."

Fangs growing and forcing my mouth open, I took a step closer to him. "Then get me in as a fighter if you have to, but get me in."

"Us," Candice said again, sounding irritated.

I turned to her. "No. Not as a fighter. You don't like fighting."

Moisture filled her eyes as they grew huge. "Sonya, Fern's in there. I have to get in." The pain in her voice got me right in the gut.

Blowing a breath out, I turned back to Owen. "Try to get us both in as spectators. But if you can't, get me in as a fighter and her as a spectator. You've felt my power. You know I qualify as exceptional."

"I can do that, if you're sure. This is a bit of a rough group," Owen said.

"I'm sure. Those seem to be the only kind I come across." Loud bird noises came from overhead, making me antsy. My new friend flew tight circles above us. Grabbing Candice's hand, I started walking again. "Call Candice with details. We're going to rest up before the big party." I couldn't keep the sarcasm out of my voice at the word 'party'. Leave it to werewolves to gather for their own fight club. Why was I not surprised?

10

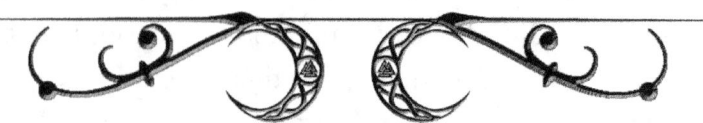

The new layer of snow that fell last night crunched beneath our boots as we walked down the road to the ranch. It was all I could do to keep my footing on the treacherous mix of ice and snow considering how sleep deprived I was.

Last night had not involved a nice hot shower and a long sleep as I had planned. My new bird friend had perched on the patio railing and made odd, and often loud, bird noises the entire night. He hadn't settled until I'd stepped back outside the next morning. All day he'd pestered me, even showing up when we went back to Fern's apartment in hopes of finding him there. No such luck. I'd gotten the very strong sense the bird wanted me to follow him because he kept flying off and back. But it was more than that.

At least now he seemed content, quiet even, as he flew slightly ahead of us, leading the way. Though I didn't want to admit it to myself last night, something connected me to him. The bird had power, not like a werewolf, different, but power nonetheless. I didn't get the feeling he was a shifter, but he was something special for sure. His power and mine felt linked in a way, and I found I could understand what he was feeling. I liked animals just as much as I liked people, more in many cases, and I understood them and their quirks. But this was more mystical than physical.

Gold and pink painted the sky above the trees as the sun hovered on the final slice of the horizon. Its beauty seemed to mock my irritable mood. Everything about this plan rubbed me the wrong way. Not bringing the Jeep had been a necessary inconvenience. Werewolves walked everywhere they could for the sake of the environment, so if I insisted on bringing the Jeep it would appear strange. But I would have loved to in case we needed an escape vehicle.

"Why didn't you wear makeup? It's a party, after all," Candice said.

"Ever since being bitten in, I can't stand the smell, the unnatural way it suffocates my skin," I said.

Head cocked, she considered me for a moment. "Yeah, I guess I get that. But it's one of those things I can't give up. It's my armor. Plus, you're lucky. You're blessed with naturally gorgeous, lush eyelashes."

A hand went automatically to brush over one of my closed eyes. "You think so? Thanks. But hey, you don't need makeup as armor. You're beautiful without it. And pop culture making you think you need to wear it to be beautiful is just oppressive patriarchy telling us we need

Heather McCorkle

129

to look a certain way to be considered up to their standards."

She laughed, but it was a triumphant sound. "All right, Sonya, throwing down the feminist gauntlet. I love it!"

We high-fived, making my bird crawk at us. Candice indicated him with a lift of her chin. "I get the feeling he's going to stick around a while. You should give him a name."

As if he knew we were talking about him, he circled around, eyeing me.

"What do you think?" I asked him. "Should I name you?"

He swooped down and landed on a branch not ten feet from me, lost his grip, scrambled, and fluttered back into the air. At great risk to my own well-being, I held out an arm in offer of a perch. To my extreme surprise, he landed on it, gripping ever so carefully with his huge talons. A few beats of his wings helped steady him, but made several of his feathers catch in my hair. He weighed a ton. If I weren't a werewolf, I didn't think I'd be able to hold him up for long.

"Holy shit!" Candice exclaimed, making him flutter his wings again.

"Ow," I said softly as he pulled more of my hair. "You're a bit clumsy, fellah."

Candice laughed. "He's a lot clumsy. And huge. By the gods, he is really huge!" She walked around him, getting a good look.

Easily over three feet from his bell-shaped tail feathers to his slightly hooked beak, he was quite big. Up close his black feathers shone like silk, catching the gold light of the sunset. Stunning amber eyes with darker streaks coming out from the middle regarded me with intelligence and what might have been affection. One of his feet didn't quite grip as strong as the other. I wondered if it were residual damage from the attack the other night. I didn't feel the taint of injury in his energy, but I also knew there were some things even our power couldn't heal, particularly if it were something a person was born with.

Just like that I knew, he had been born with a slightly deformed left foot. Us touching threw a door wide open that had only been cracked before. His power, a beautiful blue so dark it was hard to tell it was blue at first, shone around every one of his feathers.

"He's so handsome," I said, voice sounding every bit as awed as I felt.

Looking at him like this, connecting with his power, I realized I didn't need to name him. He already had one.

"His name is Gripp."

One side of her mouth cocking up and brows rising, Candice looked from the bird to me. "Gripp?"

"Yep."

"Why?" she asked, drawing the word out into two syllables, sounding genuinely puzzled, and a little judgmental.

A small bird sound came from him. I would have sworn he sounded offended.

"Hey, don't knock it. It's his name. It is what it is," I said in a defensive tone.

Hands going up, palms out, she took a step away as he lifted his wings. "Okay, okay."

Though he lowered his wings, he remained puffed up. I reached over and smoothed the feathers along his back.

"What made you choose that?" she asked.

"I didn't. It's his name." I'd heard it before, or rather, read it somewhere. The memory tickled just out of my reach.

"Did the bird tell you that?" she asked in a tone that bordered on laughter.

"In a way, yes."

Eyes widening, she took a harder look at Gripp. "Really?" She shook her head, not in disbelief, but as if marveling over the fact. "Helper of troubled werewolves, lightning rod, and now she talks to birds." Her gaze went skyward. "Really, Freya? You couldn't have spread those gifts around a little?"

A laugh escaped me, taking a good amount of tension with it.

"It's...unique," she said.

"I like it." Gripp's chest feathers puffed up and he lifted his beak.

Then it hit me. "Charles Dickens had a raven named Grip. Though I get a strong feeling my Gripp's name is spelled with two p's."

Those perfectly plucked brows of Candice's rose into the purple streak within her side bangs. "Now your bird can spell. This is just getting weirder and weirder."

"Welcome to my life."

Like we'd discussed, Owen waited at the intersection of the main road and the one leading to the ranch. Leaning against a tree, one foot propped beneath him against the trunk, he looked the picture of casual. But in black slacks and a silky blue button up shirt, he appeared ready for date night. When he laid eyes on Candice, a huge smile spread across his face. It melted the moment his gaze slid over to me.

Suspicion spider stepped along my arms. Gripp let out a little bird noise of irritation and shifted his weight on my shoulder. Damn but he was heavy, and way, way too big to be perching on my shoulder.

As we approached, Owen cleared his throat and pushed away from the tree. "You ladies look beautiful tonight," he said, blushing when he looked at Candice.

Skeptical, I narrowed my gaze at him. Just in case, I had on blue jeans so worn they looked like rats had gnawed holes in them, faded calf-high black boots, a white tank, and my favorite blue flannel over it. The only nice thing I had on was the necklace Ty had gotten me last Yule—a silver knotwork piece of a crescent moon with a raven perched on it. The irony was not lost on me. I wondered what Ty would think when he met Gripp.

"Thanks. You look pretty good yourself," Candice said without a hint of the awkwardness I would have felt at her age.

She, unlike me, had dressed to kill in a little sleeveless V-neck, black dress that hit her just above the knees and fanned out when she'd twirled back in our hotel room. In typical Candice style, she had accessorized with a black leather motorcycle jacket and a pair of lace up witchy black boots with a platform heal.

After allowing her and Owen to fawn over each other with a few more specific compliments sprinkled with giggles, I interrupted. "So you're getting us in?"

The way he swallowed hard made it obvious I wasn't going to like the answer.

"About that…" As he picked at a nail, he looked anywhere but at me.

"I have to fight," I said.

Desperation filled his widening eyes as he took a step closer to me. "I tried, I swear I did. But Boss said he had enough spectators. I got him to let

Candice in as one, but only by saying I had a special fighter for him."

"It's okay," I said.

The desperation melted into shock. "It is?"

"I'm not thrilled about the idea, but as long as Candice doesn't have to fight, we're good. Let's go get this over with."

As I thought about asking Gripp to take to the skies and make himself scarce just in case, he did exactly that. His feathers caught in my hair a little as he wobbled on the takeoff, pulling enough to elicit and "Ow," from me. He made a little bird noise of contrition in response, then disappeared into the dark branches above us—with a good amount of rustling.

"I still think you should have named him Menace," Candice teased.

I rubbed my head where a few strands of hair had pulled free. "If he didn't already have a name of his own, I wouldn't necessarily disagree."

This time the guards opened the gate wide when they saw us coming. As we walked through Ponytail looked us up and down, whistled, and shook his head. "I don't know how you landed such hotties, Mic."

Owen flinched at the name as if it stung. His power flared, but it was mid-level at best, easily beneath that of Ponytail. Little in life bothered me more than a bully. Letting out the growl building in my throat, I stepped between him and Owen.

"This hottie is his fighter, so you better show some respect," I warned.

"Psh. You? You're just a slip of a thing. I could eat you in one bite," Ponytail said.

Fangs bared, I stepped right up in his personal space and let the wall hiding my power slip just a little. It flowed over him like a lead blanket. Ponytail gasped and stepped back so quickly he slid on a spot of ice and ended up falling against the stone pillar behind him. Breath coming in short gasps, eyes gone huge and white, he looked like he wanted to crawl in a deep, dark hole and hide.

"You couldn't even get your fangs around my little finger," I said through a sneer.

From his post by the other pillar, Shaggy laughed loud and hard. "Serves you right," he eventually got out between giggles.

We walked through the gate and didn't look back. On the other side a road cut through the freshly fallen snow, winding around and into a copse of evergreens so tall they looked like they might touch the half moon rising above their pointed tops. Deep ruts dug into the snow where people had been driving, deep enough my Jeep may have bottomed out in some spots. A few feet away someone had cleared a walking path beneath the cover of deep green pine boughs. From the way snow piled against the trees in clumps, the path had clearly been made by a snow blower. Leave it to werewolves to put more care into upkeep on a walking path instead of a road. Regardless, I was grateful for it so I didn't have to walk in calf deep snow that might sneak into my boots. A good six inches had dropped over night.

"What are the rules of the matches?" I asked as we walked. Gods, I hoped there were rules.

"Pretty typical, point based system. Potentially deadly blows aren't allowed, and will not only lose a wolf the match, but get them banned," Owen explained.

On one hand that was reassuring, on the other, not so much. It probably included calling down lightning. But, considering that was a talent unique to myself and none of these wolves had seen anything like it, I didn't plan on doing it. If I had to, I supposed that meant things had gone so south it didn't matter if I lost the match or not.

"What about forms and blood?" I asked.

"A coin is flipped and the winner chooses the form, and first blood is a full point, like normal. Excessive blood can result in points taken away, though. Boss likes to keep his fighters breathing."

"Good. I like to stay breathing. How are fighters matched?" I asked.

"Boss feels out their power and matches them accordingly. And he'll know if you're hiding the full weight of your power, so I don't recommend hiding it."

Damn. That changed everything. Even now I hid my power from Owen. "Okay." I gave Candice a pointed look. "You need to wander around, try to find Fern before that point."

"Gotcha," she said with a nod.

Owen looked from Candice to me, eyes narrowing. "Why do I have the feeling there is something you aren't telling me?"

I patted him on the shoulder. "Honey, there is a lot we aren't telling you."

Glaring at me, Candice grabbed his hand. "But we want to tell you. It's just…better for you if you don't know right now."

Though his tight browed look suggested he disagreed, he didn't let go of her hand.

From somewhere in the darkness overhead, Gripp let out a long and emphatic, "Crawk!" Deep down in my center, I knew it for what it was, a call to follow.

In the near distance, I heard a small crowd of people laughing and chatting. The feel of their collective power reached me. Amidst all that power I felt the somewhat tumultuous energy of the troubled newly bitten. It worried at me like a seed stuck between my teeth. And it drew me like north draws a compass needle. Thankfully, we were heading in that general direction. Beside me, Candice and Owen chatted aimlessly about their interests and hobbies, but with my attention focused elsewhere I barely heard the conversation.

The sounds of revelers carried to my ears, growing louder as we went. Behind the slight hill we walked up, a flickering yellow glow emanated. I didn't smell or hear a bonfire, but it was definitely fire, making me think maybe propane firepits or something. Beneath the reveling came grunts of effort, groans of pain, and the slap of flesh on flesh.

"They've started the fights already," I said.

"No official matches, just people warming up. I told Boss you'd be mid-level. I hope that's right," Owen said.

"Something like that," I said. My physical fighting skills were definitely mid-level at best, but with the alpha command I could use, and the lightning calling, well, I didn't exactly know where that put me.

Seeing my guarded expression, Owen waved a hand. "No worries. He'll check all new entrants prior to the fight so if you're higher, he can bump you up."

The excitement and hint of hope in his voice made me wonder what he got out of bringing in a new fighter. No doubt a cut of any betting that occurred. I respected that he didn't press me on my abilities, though. From the way he described his boss, the man didn't sound like he was forcing people to fight, or keeping them against their will. But I couldn't be sure without meeting the guy.

We crested the hill and started down it. The road continued into a valley in which sat a large A-frame style house at the edge of the forest. In front of it stretched a field of green with a raised fighting ring at its center. It looked for all intents and purposes like a boxing ring, with four corners and ropes stretched between the uprights. Light glowed from at least a dozen tall propane firepits, the kind meant to stand around, all throughout the field. Sixty or so people gathered around the fighting ring, every one of them werewolves from the feel of the power emanating off them. A few wolves sat around the outer edge of the crowd, back near the trees as if they weren't quite comfortable enough to mingle, but wanted to be there regardless.

Among all of them, I couldn't find the troubled newly bitten. They had disappeared or somehow their power had become hidden. I didn't like the implications of the second option. A newly bitten could no more hide their own power than they could control their wolf. Which meant, if option number two were the case, someone else had suppressed their power.

In the ring, two figures in human form—clothed, thank goodness—exchanged blows. To my surprise, their fists were wrapped like those of boxers. Most werewolves didn't bother with such precautions. These two were clearly lower-level fighters, keeping to one form, and not growing claws or fangs. Still, the fight possessed the brutality and aggression of full contact. Heads snapped back from the impact of punches, blood flew from mouths, and growls of anger issued from the combatants. This 'boss' of Owen's might not condone killing, but clearly he didn't mind his fighters getting beaten and bloodied.

Great.

Carefully checking the walls around my power for chinks, I straightened my shoulders and tried to walk with more confidence. To pull this off, I had to look the part as much as possible.

Owen walked with a bit of a strut as he led us right into the crowd. People's eyes widened as they turned to look at him, then Candice and myself. I got the distinct impression he didn't often get to be the popular guy. As we moved deeper into the crowd, they began to turn and part for us. Whistles and catcalls followed in our wake. I did my best to exude an off the market vibe with my resting bitch face and refusal to meet anyone's gaze. It only made the catcalls worse.

A bell dinged over the noise and the fighters in the ring separated and retreated to opposite corners. A man not much taller than me ducked between the ropes and strode into the center of the ring. Long, black hair pulled back in a topknot exposed a clean-shaven, oval face with a strong jaw and a slightly crooked nose. A faded scar cut through his right eyebrow. Despite his size, the energy of a very powerful alpha exuded from him. The fighters gravitated to him without a word being said. He took one of each of their hands in his, stared out at the crowd for a long, dramatic moment, then thrust the hand of the fighter on his right into the air.

"Duncan is the winner!" he announced. He slapped both fighters companionably on the back. "Good fight, men, good fight." I detected a very distinct Chinese accent. He sounded like second generation American at the most, and one who had likely grown up in a predominately Chinese speaking home.

The strength of his power meant I wouldn't be able to hide my power from him for long, if at all. So we had to hurry this up.

I leaned in close to Candice. "Do you smell him anywhere?"

"Yeah," she said in a far-off voice.

Looking down, I followed her gaze. She stared at the fighters in the ring, now shaking hands.

"That's him, the loser of the fight," she whispered.

The winner danced around the ring to the cheering of the crowd, while the loser—Fernando, apparently—ducked between the ropes and jumped down to the ground. We made a V-line in his direction. Calling out words of protest that became swallowed in the noise, Owen followed. My skin crawled as the power of so many strange werewolves pushed at me from all sides. It made me want to extend my fangs and claws, to fight or flee, but I resisted.

We caught up to Fernando at the edge of the crowd, heading toward a barn with a woodpile before it tucked into the trees on the right side of the house. Candice grabbed his arm and turned him toward her.

"Thanks, but I don't want any company tonight—oh. Candice. Wow. Um, what are you doing here?" he asked, eyes popping open wide.

Bronze skinned and baby-faced, with a mop of sweaty black bangs hanging over one eye, he was adorable in a Latino boy band sort of way. The purple and red spreading out from his other eye gave him a rakish look that hardened him. One hand held the ribs on his right side.

"Checking on you, fool. You haven't called or texted me in two weeks, which is totally not like you. I thought something had happened. Are you okay?" Candice asked, voice breaking on the last question, her hands going toward him.

Glaring, he waved as if brushing her off. "Yeah, I'm fine," he snapped.

Face going blank, eyes hard, she straightened, pulling her hand back from him.

The lines between his brows smoothed and his grimace of irritation fell. "Sorry, Can. I just lost a match so I'm a little testy."

She shook her hair about her and put on a smile. "I get it. It's okay. But hey, on our last call I saw the bruises on your face, and then when you didn't reach out again, I got worried," she pressed in a firm tone that made me proud.

Beckoning for her to follow, he walked over and sat down on a fallen log a few feet away. We all followed, Owen and I hanging back just a little. While I got that they probably wanted privacy, my need to ensure he was here of his own free will overrode that. The sound of wind moving across feathers told me Gripp soared just overhead. The rustle of pine boughs and a few squawks told me he'd landed in the tree above us. Nothing came crashing down, so I figured he must have found his balance. Candice glared up into the boughs and braced.

A groan of pain slipped from him as Fernando shifted on the log, one hand clutching at his ribs. "Sorry. I didn't mean to worry you. I just got busy with matches," he said.

Candice sat down beside him, far enough away it wasn't intimate, but close enough to reach him, as if she were afraid he'd dash away. "Why are you fighting?" she asked.

"I make enough money to live off of," he said.

Jaw clenching, Candice sat up ramrod straight. "Seriously? Because you need money? You aren't in trouble are you? You don't owe this ringmaster guy or whoever he is money, do you?" she asked. The growl in her voice made me take a step in their direction. I lingered close by in the shadows, just in case.

"No, it's not like that. The money is a bonus, really. Fighting…it helps with the restlessness, the need to hunt," he said the last part in a whisper.

Shoulders lowering, Candice put a hand on his knee. "Oh. I get it."

I hated to interrupt, but I had to know. "What about the others? Are they here of their free will?" I asked.

Gaze rising to meet mine, he shook his head as if confused by my presence. "Who are you?"

A gong rang out over the reply I'd been about to give, the sound reverberating off the trees, amplified somehow throughout the valley.

Owen stepped in front of me, looking like he wanted to touch my arm, but wasn't sure he should. "That's our call. But since you found your friend, you don't have to fight if you don't want to," he said.

Remembering how much he had puffed up when we'd walked through the crowd made my decision for me. "A deal's a deal." Besides, I still needed to find the troubled werewolf.

His eyes grew comically huge and his smile rivalled that of a crazed villain, only filled with joy instead of menace.

I turned to Candice. "You gonna be all right here?"

"Yeah, thanks," she said.

"Lead the way," I told Owen. Since Fernando didn't seem inclined to talk to me, I could find out the answer to my question elsewhere.

Some of the joy leached from Owen's face when he looked back at Candice and Fernando. "I hope I'll see you later?" he made it a question.

Warmth radiated from the huge smile she gave him. "Definitely."

With that, Owen turned and led the way with so much bounce in his step I feared he might fly up into the sky sans umbrella and start singing. It was a good thing he was excited enough for both of us, because I was feeling none of it. But, I needed to meet his boss and ask him a few very direct questions about this werewolf weekend entertainment he had set up.

"Liang is a fair man, and he'll make sure not to put you in a weight class that is too much for you," Owen said.

"Liang?"

"Boss."

I hid a smile and nodded.

Owen didn't take me to the ring like I thought he would. Instead, we walked toward the house where a group of fifteen or so people stood gathered on the front deck. From out of a set of huge French doors, came the Chinese man I'd seen lift the hand of the winning fighter in the ring. He rubbed his hands together as he strode up to the group.

"All right, then. Middle weight sorting time. Is this all our middle weight fighters?" he asked in a voice that carried deep into the night, even above the noise of the larger crowd behind us—alpha projection was what I'd come to call it. The skill was usually something I'd only seen in alphas of packs. It made me wonder, and worry, about this guy's history.

Following Owen, I walked up the steps onto the deck and stood at the back of the group. With a wink and a thumbs up, he jumped back down onto the ground into the steadily growing crowd of onlookers. Among them I saw a few bookies starting to accept money from people and jot down their information on notepads.

Shifter power flowed through the air before me, drawing my attention back to where Liang stood before my group. His power emanated from him to envelop a man, testing and probing at his. It felt somewhat like a hot pressure front moving around a warm one. It made my own power want to rise and push against it, but I held back.

Liang nodded to the man. "Mid weight." He pointed to the left and the guy walked over to stand where directed.

The next person Liang evaluated, a tall woman with more muscle in one arm than I had in my entire body, made him shake his head. "Heavy weight." He pointed to the right.

Giving him a coy smile that looked very out of place on her, she shrugged and walked over to stand on the right. Liang methodically worked his way through those gathered, evaluating them and directing them to the right or left based on what he felt in their power. With each one he grew closer to me. While he was otherwise occupied, I scanned the crowd with my extra sense, trying desperately to find the troubled newly bitten before the jig was up. I held onto the miniscule hope that maybe Gripp would alert me to the person's presence. But, he only stood at the peak of the A-frame house, a dark shadow against a dark blue sky, head moving as he scanned the surroundings.

Finally, with no other fighters left, Liang stood before me. Dammit. Still no sign of the troubled werewolf to be. The one squinty eye, other brow raised look Liang gave me made it clear he knew I had walls up.

"You are the fighter Owen brought in," he said.

"I am."

Still no sign. The time on my deadline clicked down to the last second.

"Well, I have to feel your power to verify your weight class. If you don't let me gauge it, you don't get to fight. Do you want to fight?" he asked.

I most certainly did not. But, I hoped if I did, it might call the troubled one to me. "Yes," I said, and let my walls down.

Gasping, Liang rocked back on his heels. On instinct, I reached out and he clasped my hand, catching himself before he could teeter over. Couldn't have the ringleader losing face in front of everyone. That would be a sure-fire way to guarantee this night went downhill. We stood like that for several moments, hands clasped, Liang staring wide-eyed at me. Silence fell over those gathered on the deck with us. It slowly spread out across the field.

"I've never felt a power like yours. Who are you?" he demanded.

At this point, I saw no reason to lie. "Sonya Michaelson."

Gasps erupted from those gathered on the deck.

He dropped my hand like it was on fire and took a step back. "Seeker!" The reverence in his voice combined with the shocked look on his face warned me he was about to drop to a knee and expose his neck to me—a very annoying thing too many werewolves did when they found out who I was. Using my werewolf speed, I snatched his hand back up and gave it just enough of a tug to ensure he didn't kneel.

"Please don't," I whispered.

Head tilting slightly, he gazed at me for a long moment. I felt that same pressure of evaluation of power he'd done on the others, but it also felt like he looked inside, at my desires. "Did you really come here to fight?" he asked, tone curious. "I don't have any fighters at your level, but…" His gaze went off into the darkness as he contemplated.

Since he seemed beyond the whole embarrassing kneeling thing, I let go of his hand. "No. I came looking for someone. Can we talk somewhere more private?" I asked, deciding to go with a partial truth. He didn't need to know we'd come here looking for Fernando.

"Yes, of course." He turned to the mid-weight fighters now hovering on the edge of the deck looking like they might flee. "Fighters, stretch and warm up. The matches will continue when I return," he said in an upbeat tone that showed none of the anxiety lingering in the creases around his eyes.

With a wave of his hand, he invited me to walk with him toward the house. I checked the crowd for Candice. She still sat with Fernando near the barn. Our eyes met and she nodded, letting me know she was okay. I turned and followed Liang. Those gathered on the deck flowed away from us with impressive werewolf speed. From the looks of shock, and fear in some cases, on their faces, I wouldn't have to worry about fighting anyone.

Before stepping across the threshold into Liang's house, I reached out with my extra sense for the troubled newly bitten once more. I thought I caught an inkling of a feeling, but it faded like whisps of fog on a windy day. A glance at the rooftop showed Gripp perched comfortably and looking half asleep. I stepped inside and closed the door behind me.

Wood tones, animal hides, and warm colors decorated the open concept home with it's incredibly high ceiling that seemed to go on forever. We'd walked into a living room with a huge, stone fireplace dominating one wall around which furniture gathered. Liang motioned to the couch and chairs.

"Please, sit, make yourself comfortable. Is there anything I can get you? A drink, food?" he offered, sounding flustered.

I waved a hand. "No. Please, you don't need to go out of your way. I didn't mean to surprise you by showing up like this, but I never know how people are going to take me being in their territory, so I try to keep a low profile until I can't anymore."

He sat on the arm of the couch, scratching at his chin. "You thought I might deny you an audience." His eyes narrowed. "It's more than that."

In answer I lifted my brows, pursed my lips, and tilted my head.

"You were suspicious of my operation."

"After a chat with my friend, seeing his bruises and black eye, he went dark for a while. I had to be sure nothing had happened to him and that he was here of his own free will," I said.

"You thought I might be forcing people to fight for profit," Liang said as if this were something people often thought. It made me think I wasn't the first person who'd come looking for a missing friend or loved one.

"You have to admit, it seemed suspicious."

"But you found your friend and they are fine." This too, he said as if it were a conversation he'd had many times before.

"They seem to be."

He sighed but smiled at the end of it. "But you still have your doubts. I get it, but you have the wrong impression. Wolves come to me from all over, those who don't want to belong to a pack."

His easy tone and relaxed mannerisms soothed me enough that I walked over and sat on the chair opposite him.

He went on. "You see, most of us still have an instinctual need to fight for our place in a pack, even if we don't want to belong to one. I offer these wolves an outlet, a way to satisfy that instinct that keeps them out of trouble. I don't allow fights to the death, or even blows that seriously injure. Anyone who breaks those rules I cast out, or in the extreme cases, turn over to the Caninus Council."

From everything I'd learned about werewolves so far, it made perfect sense. But one thing still bothered me. "It seems you are doing a good thing here. But I felt a troubled newly bitten, one on the verge of losing their battle with madness, somewhere out in that crowd."

Wrinkles formed around his pursed mouth and at the corners of his eyes. "It happens sometimes, newly bitten who haven't turned yet come here because they've been abandoned by the one who bit them in. I help them if I can."

"You don't think any of your people would have bit them in?" I asked.

"Definitely not. There aren't many of us here, which allows me to keep them all in line much easier than what you're used to in Hemlock Hollow."

Ouch. The dig cut deep. But he wasn't wrong. The ones who had been biting in werewolves without the council's permission had come from Hemlock Hollow where the pack sizes numbered in the hundreds.

"I'm not from Hemlock Hollow. I don't belong to one of their packs, though not from their lack of trying," I growled out the last part.

His eyes widened in surprise. "Oh, I just thought…"

"I know. Everyone does. Its usually safer for me to allow them to think that."

"You're a lone wolf then?"

Gaze going to the exposed wooden beams in his house, I pursed my lips as I thought about Ty, Ayra, and Vidar. "Not exactly. But officially, yes."

Some tension I hadn't realized he'd been holding onto eased from Liang on an exhale. His face smoothed and his shoulders dropped. "An interesting answer," he said with a smile.

"Do you have a pen and paper? I'll give you my number in case any troubled ones come to you who need a little extra help," I suggested.

"I'm not sure I'd consider finding them to hand them over to the reaper is considered help," he said in a skeptical tone.

Brows furrowing, I stared at him for a moment, gathering the right words. "That isn't what I do. I try to find them before they shift for the first time and guide them to make peace with their wolf so they don't go mad when they do shift."

He regarded me for a long moment, his power perusing my own. "You're telling the truth."

"Of course I am. I didn't spend years in med school, and weeks in psychology classes to hand people over to a death sentence without even trying to help them," I said.

Slowly, a smile spread across his lips. "In that case, definitely."

Through the extremely good insulation of the house I barely heard Gripp's frantic "Crawk!"

Urgency took root deep in my gut and yanked me to my feet. A moment later, I felt the pull of the troubled newly bitten and I knew without a doubt, Gripp was calling me to hunt them.

"How do you feel about me seeking out a troubled newly bitten on your land?" I asked, every muscle tense, barely able to restrain myself.

"Of course. Do what you need to do to help them," Liang said.

Feeling my rising power, he got to his feet. But I wasn't able to wait for him to see me out. At another cry from Gripp, I took off running for the front door.

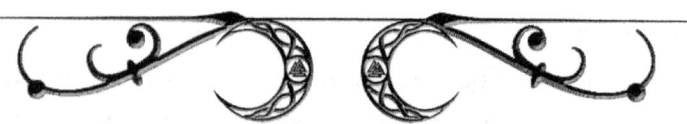

11

Dozens had gathered just beyond the deck, waiting to see what would happen when Liang and I emerged. From the surprised looks on their faces, they didn't expect me to come bolting out of the door. Thankfully, shock rendered them frozen for a moment, giving me time to leap over their heads and hit the ground some twenty feet behind them running. The moment I emerged Gripp took to the air, shooting like an arrow straight for the forest beyond the fighting ring. I followed, leaping over firepits and people.

Candice called out something to me but I didn't have time to stop and answer any questions. This troubled was a skittish one and if they got away from me now, I might never find them. I could run faster in wolf form, but if I shifted, I'd tear my clothes out and destroy them. Going back to find Candice, naked amidst almost a hundred strange werewolves, did not sound fun. Plus, I loved these boots. So I ran with everything I had in me.

Seconds later, I left the valley behind that the house sat in. Cedar boughs whipped at my arms and face, ferns snagged at my legs, but I pushed through it all, letting the energy of the troubled one draw me.

The distance between us closed foot by foot. I heard them running ahead of me, maybe thirty yards away. But not having shifted yet, their power wasn't fully developed, meaning they were slower. Thirty yards became twenty, then ten. I saw them through the trees, a silhouette against the darkness, their power outlining them in a purplish pink aura visible only to supernaturals.

"Wait, please. I've come to help you!" I called out.

With a glance over their shoulder, they slowed. Not wanting to scare them off, so did I.

"You're scared, having trouble with all the instincts rising in you. I can help," I called out.

Breathing heavy, they stopped and leaned against a tree. I stopped as well. Thirty feet seemed like a good buffer to keep them calm. I didn't want to press my luck. Little bird noises that sounded as if they were supposed to be soothing, came from above.

"Thank you Freya for not letting him fall on them," I whispered.

"What?" the person asked, a young woman.

Clearly she already had the super werewolf hearing.

"I really can help," I said.

She made a snorting sound of disagreement. "No one can help me."

"Not true," I disagreed.

Now leaning heavily against the tree, she turned toward me. "You're that seeker, which means the reaper isn't far behind, and if you can't help me, she's coming next."

"She isn't here. And it won't come to that," I said with complete confidence. I felt her internal struggle, a darkening of her power, but it was mild, only a few shades, easily recoverable if she was willing to try. And the fact she had stopped running and now engaged in conversation told me she was willing.

"You sound so sure," she said with a healthy dose of sarcasm in a tone that made me think she was probably under twenty-five.

"I am. I can feel it in your power, the potential, the strength of will. You can get through this."

Sniffling, she took a few steps toward me, putting a hand out on a closer tree. "Really?" This time her voice held no hint of sarcasm.

"Really." I took a few steps in her direction, then sat on a tree stump.

"But I'm going to become a monster."

"No, you're not. The thing inside feels wild, powerful, like it's going to overwhelm you, but the opposite is true," I said.

She walked closer, stopping no more than twenty feet away now. "The opposite?"

"If you embrace the wolf within, it will free you. You'll still be able to think. You'll still be you, only powerful, fast, and a part of something bigger than you ever imagined."

"A part of something?" She walked right up and sat before me on the ground.

High cheekbones and bright hazel eyes peeked out from behind messy pink hair that barely touched her shoulders. A grey sweatshirt two sizes too big and baggy jeans, both likely donated or stolen, made her look small and fragile.

"Yes, the earth. You'll feel a connection to it unlike anything you've ever felt before. Sounds hokey, but I swear, it's true."

"But the movies, the books, they depict werewolves as monsters," she said.

Now I made a snort of derision. "Lies. Both kill, but humans are the real monsters. Humans take from the earth, pollute her, and cover her with suffocating concrete and asphalt, all for our own gain. Wolves live in harmony with nature, giving and taking in equal measure, supporting the planet. Which sounds like a monster to you?"

Some of the moisture began to disappear from her eyes and she regarded me with a sense of wonder. "I never thought of it that way. The guy who bit me didn't tell me anything. Jerk took off right after."

I had to swallow down my anger. "Did you consent to being bitten in?" I asked gently.

Looking down, she picked at a loose string on her jeans. "Yes. But he said he'd stay with me, help me through the change. Then I had trouble, got freaked out, and he bailed."

"Well, what made you consent?" I asked, sensing she teetered on the edge and knowing it was best to stick to the positive part of what she'd said.

"Being strong, fast, living five lifetimes."

"That's all true."

Hope shone on her face when she looked up at me. "Can you help me get through the change?"

Warmth spread through my chest. "Absolutely."

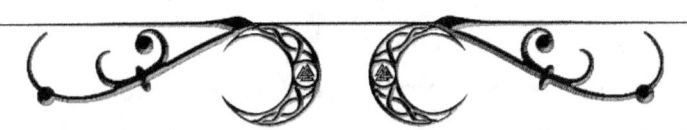

12

On the way back home to Missoula, Candice surprised me by looking through the apartment listings of a rental website. While stopped at a diner for grub, at my encouragement, she registered us with the site and we put in an application. The place wasn't great, but it was worlds above the dive I lived in now, and it was bigger. Her excitement made me happier than anything else, though. According to her we would have girls' movie night each week, taco night, and a decorating shopping spree at a thrift store.

All the while, the troubled newly bitten, Rio—short for Catriona—sat in the back seat with Gripp. The huge bird had absolutely insisted on getting in when I did. Satisfied, he had perched on the back seat, making his odd bird noises now and again when Rio told him how pretty of a bird he was. I said more than one silent prayer to Odin not to let him poop in my Jeep.

When we reached Ty's place in Missoula, he made us lunch. While Candice and Rio chatted and ate, Ty and I stepped out onto the back deck. The peekaboo view of the cerulean blue lake through the fragrant pine trees soothed away the stress of the last few weeks. This was my happy place, mostly because of the hot blond guy standing next to me, but the view didn't hurt either. We leaned against the deck railing. Our elbows touched and I laid my head on his shoulder. Gripp perched on the railing on my opposite side, so close if I moved a few inches, I'd knock him off.

We stood like that, staring out at the view, for several long moments. Tension sang through Ty's power. My own picked up on the discordant tune, leaving me feeling like something buzzed under my skin. Gripp kept making a weird noise that wasn't helping.

"I should have given you all the details of what we were doing up front," I finally said to break the tension.

Lines digging deep furrows between his blond brows, Ty turned to me and put a hand on my arm. "No. That is not what I am brooding about." Sighing, he ran a hand through his chin length blond hair, making me long to touch it, to touch him, despite the tension.

"Well don't leave me hanging. The suspense is killing me."

"I am struggling with my fear. You are the seeker. You will have to seek out troubled shifters who need your help. I know that, and I support you in it. But it is dangerous and that scares me."

I opened my mouth to interrupt, but he gently squeezed my arm.

He went on. "You do not need to tell me where you are at every moment, or what you are doing. I trust you to know when you need help. You called me when you got nervous, and I feel like that is progress. So, I am trying to be progressive as well. It just is not easy."

Partly because I couldn't speak around the lump in my throat, but mostly because I wanted to touch him more, I picked up his hand and kissed his knuckles. "You're amazing, and I love you."

A delicious growl rumbled through his chest as he pulled me into his arms. The look of desire and affection glowing in his baby blues banished the stress of the past few days. He bent to kiss me but a loud "Crawk!" made us pull apart.

"Attention hog," I muttered.

Letting me go, he leaned over the railing to get a better look at my bird. "So this is Gripp."

At his name, Gripp made a popping sound.

I lifted my head. "Yep. What do you think, is he the result of the ritual I did with the other seeker in the astral realm?" I asked.

He nodded. "Definitely. You said he led you to Catriona?"

"Definitely."

"It makes sense that Odin would send you a raven," he said.

So he *was* a raven. "What is the real difference between a crow and a raven?" I asked.

Ty's arm slid around my waist. Gripp's head cocked to the side as he regarded us and made an odd gurgling sound. I couldn't tell if he approved or disapproved of Ty's attention. The conflicted feel of his power made me think he wasn't sure.

"See his tail there, how it fans out into a bell shape?" Ty's breath tickled my ear, sending naughty tingles all through me.

I nodded.

"That is one of the ways you can tell." That delicious, deep voice whispering in my ear made me want to wriggle against him. Too bad the girls were on the other side of the glass doors. He whispered something in Icelandic. I didn't quite catch it, but it sounded sexy as hell.

"Hmmm?" I inquired.

"They are the eyes or ears of Odin," he said.

The stories my dad used to tell me tickled at my memory. "Hugin and Munin, Odin's ravens," I whispered.

Gripp let out another "Crawk," that drew my attention. He beat his wings and stood taller, but didn't take off. For a moment he and Ty just looked at each other. Their power danced around one another like coffee and Irish creamer. A slow, big smile spread across Ty's face. At the same time,

Gripp's glossy black feathers lay down flat and his wings tucked in. Realizing they had just accepted one another, I released a breath and some pent up tension.

"I am glad you have him," Ty said.

A much more comfortable silence fell between us. I more than halfway expected him to try to talk me out of moving in with Candice, but he didn't. Moving closer, he put one arm around me and rested the other on the railing next to mine. He felt so good—warm, comforting, scintillating.

I rubbed the back of his arm. "I guess no welcome home sex unless we don't mind the Gods watching, and the girls being on the other side of those doors," I said.

Leaning in close, Ty hummed against my neck, making me shiver. "We can go for a walk where the girls will not hear," he said in a tone so filled with desire it made my insides throb. "And, I am sure the gods will not mind." The disappointment in his tone matched my own. I'd missed him, a lot.

I chuckled. "I'm starting to like these Gods more and more."

Continue reading in **Coyote Calling**, the first full-length novel in the Shifter Seeker series, releasing in August of 2022 from City Owl Press. In the meantime, if you haven't read the Children of Fenrir series, now is the perfect time! See the opening pages of this novella for a list of the recommended reading order.

If you enjoyed the read, I would be eternally grateful for a review on retail sites like Amazon. Not only does it help other readers, but it helps the retailer decide how much attention to give the book, and alternative rights such as foreign publishers, movie, television, and other media look at how many reviews books have when they are considering them. Waxing poetic, or long narratives aren't necessary if that isn't your thing. Short and sweet can help just as much!

GLOSSARY

Jötnar: race of frost giants from Jötunheimr

Seðr: magic

Vaettir: spirits

Varúlfur: werewolf

Verða: the becoming, the process of turning into a werewolf up to and including their first shifting during a full moon.

Völva: seer, medium

ACKNOWLEDGEMENTS

I'd love to thank Lisa Gayle Green and E.J. Wenstrom who helped me polish this novella until it shone. You ladies are the best!

To readers old and new, I cannot thank you enough for reading. You are the blood that keeps my creative heart pumping. Entertaining you brings me so much joy. And to my newfound BookTok community, you wonderful people blow me away each and every day with how supportive and uplifting you are. I am honored to count myself among you.

ABOUT THE AUTHOR

When she's not writing, Heather can be found on the slopes, the hiking trails, or paddleboarding. As a native Oregonian, she enjoys the outdoors nearly as much as the worlds she creates. No need to travel to the Great Northwest, though, you can find Heather on social media and her personal site.

http://www.heathermccorkle.com/

www.ingramcontent.com/pod-product-compliance
Lightning Source LLC
Chambersburg PA
CBHW061235170626
46809CB00007B/2694

* 9 7 8 1 9 3 9 4 6 9 0 7 6 *